SOUND OF *Rejoicing*

SOUND OF *Rejoicing*

Restored

Part 7

Mary E. Hanks

www.maryehanks.com

Suzanne D. Williams Cover Design:

www.feelgoodromance.com

Cover photos:

svetikd @ istockphoto.com

S_Photo @ shutterstock.com

Visit Mary's website:

www.maryehanks.com

You can write Mary at

maryhanks@maryehanks.com.

For Kathy

My sister-in-law and high school friend.

Thanks for making some fun memories

with me over the years.

For Jason

Here's to making the next decade spectacular!

hugs & kisses

Mercy, peace and love be yours in abundance.

Jude 1:2

Basalt Bay Residents

Paisley Grant – Daughter of Paul and Penny Cedars

Judah Grant – Son of Edward and Bess Grant

Paige Cedars – Paisley's younger sister/mom to Piper

Peter Cedars – Paisley' older brother/fishing in Alaska

Paul Cedars – Paisley's dad/widower

Edward Grant – Mayor of Basalt Bay/Judah's dad

Bess Grant – Judah's mom/Edward's wife

Aunt Callie – Paisley's aunt/Paul's sister

Maggie Thomas – owner of Beachside Inn

Bert Jensen – owner of Bert's Fish Shack

Mia Till – receptionist at C-MER

Craig Masters – Judah's supervisor at C-MER

Mike Linfield – Judah's boss at C-MER

Lucy Carmichael – Paisley's high school friend

Brian Corbin – Sheriff's deputy

Kathleen Baker – newcomer to Basalt Bay

Bill Sagle – pastor

Geoffrey Carnegie – postmaster/local historian

Casey Clemons – floral shop owner

Patty Lawton – hardware store owner

Brad Keifer – fisherman/school chum of Peter's

James Weston – Paul's neighbor

Sal Donovan – souvenir shop owner

Fred Buckley – council member

Sue Taylor – council member

Penny Cedars – Paisley's mom/deceased

One

Peter Cedars leaned against the doorway to the planning room in the project house, silently watching Ruby as she stared at one black-and-white photograph after another. He loved her beautiful red hair, her sparkling green eyes, and her sweet smile.

If only she stared at him as intensely as she gazed at those photos from a bygone era. His thoughts roamed back to the first inklings of romance and love between them. What, five-and-a-half years ago? How he gazed into her eyes like he could do so for ten hours straight and not tire of it. How she smiled and laughed with him as if their hearts were already knit together.

What would it take for her to want him back as her husband as much as he wanted her for his wife? It seemed like forever since they held each other and kissed like a married couple. When had she left him? Almost six weeks ago. Did he ruin everything because of his stubbornness and pride? His determination to have things his own way?

He groaned.

Ruby glanced up. "Peter. I didn't hear you come upstairs."

"Hey." He stood taller. "How's it going?"

"Good. How long have you been standing there?"

"Not long."

He wouldn't mind leaning against the doorframe for an hour imagining him and Ruby and how they loved each other in the past. Wishing for more of the same now. If he could turn back time, he'd return to their first year of marriage and do some things differently. Not in the first couple of months. That was a blissful time. But after the honeymoon phase ended, he reverted to acting almost like a bachelor. Not interacting with her like a sweetheart. A wife.

So many regrets. Lost opportunities. What were the chances of them starting over? Trying again?

"What's on your mind?" She peered up at him like she was trying to decipher his thoughts.

He coughed. Was she ready to hear what was on his mind? Was he brave enough to tell her every bit of what he'd been thinking lately? "Got any plans for today?" he asked instead.

She held up a photo of a woman in a 50's getup. "I'm trying to figure out what to do with these pictures I found in the attic. I'd like to find a family member to return them to."

"Want some help?"

"I'd love some." She pushed out a chair with her foot.

Her welcoming smile triggered the same response from him. Hopeful of what the day ahead might hold for them, he dropped into the seat opposite her, his gaze locked on hers. "Would you be interested in a beach walk with me later?"

"Sure. But isn't it stormy out?"

"Never stopped us before. Best time for beach walking, right?"

"I guess it is. Us, raingear, and a walk on the seashore. What could be better?"

"Exactly." He liked her saying, "us" first as if she was already prioritizing them in her thoughts.

They spent a half hour poring over the pictures. Peter enjoyed spending time with Ruby, hearing her laughter and voice. Just being with her made his world feel more normal.

"I wonder why the owners left these photographs behind." She frowned. "It's hard to imagine they were left intentionally."

"They were in the attic. Must have been overlooked."

She tossed a few more pictures onto the discard pile and yawned. "I think I'm ready for that walk."

"Me too." He jumped to his feet.

Downstairs, they donned raincoats and were soon traipsing along the path toward the roar of the ocean. Peter let the scents of the sea air fill him, satisfying his senses. The sound of the waves pounding the shore drew him closer, almost as if they were calling to him.

An unexpected yearning for the *Lily Forever* hit him—the sway of the deck beneath his feet, the smells of the ocean air wafting into the galley, sleeping on their bed below deck. He hadn't been away from his troller for so long before. His heart suddenly raced like something might be wrong with his fishing boat. Was an internal alert telling him something problematic might be happening in Alaska, and he wasn't there to take care of it?

He gulped. Then he met his wife's puzzled gaze. Her soft smile. His chest muscles unclenched. Surely, he was over-reacting. Everything was fine.

He would not rush back to Ketchikan without finishing what he started here. He and Ruby were on a journey to making things right between them. He didn't know how that path would look, how many twists and turns it would take, but he was determined to put his all into the effort. To be here in Basalt Bay with the woman he loved meant everything to him and their future lives together.

Now, how could he express those thoughts to her?

Two

Ruby caught Peter staring at her as they strode across the pebbly beach. His look was so tender, she couldn't glance away, couldn't break the tenuous tie suspended between them. Did he want to say something to her? Something he hadn't been able to express yet?

If only he talked to her like they did in the beginning, really sharing their hearts. Sometimes when he gazed at her, she saw her Peter from five years ago. She missed the man who'd won her over with hours of conversation. And those deep, powerful kisses of his. She missed those too.

They'd been walking for twenty minutes, the rain pelting them hard one minute, then changing to a soft mist resembling butterfly kisses the next. They occasionally bantered back and forth, but mostly they walked, hand in hand, simply talking about ordinary things. Sometimes sharing a memory.

"Remember the night the Aurora Borealis was out so bright it looked like a neon light show?" "Do you recall that two-hundred pound halibut I caught?" "Remember the first night we slept on the Lily Forever?"

She liked this part of their lives together—her, Peter, and the outdoor elements. This was the way they'd lived on the boat for their five years of marriage. Well, not the part about holding hands and gazing into each other's eyes. That romantic sizzle had been sadly missing. But in the beginning, their relationship was like this.

Why was Peter acting so attentive and shiny-eyed toward her today? Her pleasure in the gentle way he held her hand, and in the way he acted like he was so into her, deteriorated into concern. Did he hope to coax her into returning to Alaska sooner than he'd planned? What if he suggested they leave before Christmas? That was only a week and a half away. She wasn't ready for that.

They hadn't even worked things out between them like they still needed to do. She withdrew her fingers from his clasp, tucking them into her raincoat pocket, and put some space between them. With each footfall of her boots, her heels dug deeper into the wet sand, and her emotions dug deeper into worrying.

"Rube?" His deep tones rumbled over her. "What's wrong? What did I say?"

She groaned, half wanting to keep her thoughts to herself, half wanting to be totally honest. Honesty won out. "I love that you're spending time with me. Beach walking in the rain and holding hands are some of my favorite things to do in the whole world."

"I remember." He stepped ahead of her and put his hands on her shoulders, bringing her to a stop. "I like holding your hand and being with you. Is there something wrong with that?"

"No. Only—"

"Are you questioning why I'm spending time with my wife?" A soft smile crossed his mouth, his white teeth framed by his reddish beard.

"I just—" A breath caught in her throat. "Maybe." Her heart danced to some weird rhythm she didn't recognize. He said he liked holding her hand and being with her. That was sweet of him. "Why are you being so gentle and caring with me today?"

"Because I'm trying to find my way back to you." His hands moved from her shoulders down to her wrists in slow increments. "Back to our love." The wind snagged his words and tossed them into the air, almost out of her hearing. "I miss being close to you. Having you in my arms."

Even with those words, she had to ask, "This isn't about your leaving, is it?"

"Leaving? Where would I go?" Another smile crossed his face, his mouth getting perilously close to hers.

She licked her lower lip, swiping rainwater away with her tongue. Not as an invitation. Yet Peter's gaze zeroed in on her lips. She swallowed four or five times.

Then somehow—either she stepped forward, or he tugged her to him—she was snuggled in his embrace, his beard-lined mouth pressing softly against hers, their lips moving together with a simmering heat and passion she hadn't felt in eons.

Oh, Peter.

His arms wrapped around her more fully, her body melding against his, rain slicker against rain slicker. And his mouth ... oh, goodness ... his mouth caressed her lips, her cheeks, her neck, then her mouth again. His ticklish whiskers brushed against her skin, heating her up even more. Steam rose around them in the rain. But not one inch of her was chilled.

"Rube?"

His hoarse voice yanked her from the pleasure of kissing him. She inched back, blinking against the raindrops clinging to her lashes, gazing into his dazed-looking eyes—or maybe the dazed eyes were hers. His hands clasped hers like he wouldn't let her get too far from him.

"I know this doesn't solve everything between us," he said in a husky tone. He seemed to be trying to catch his breath. "But it's a start, right?" His eyes stared hungrily at her like he wanted to pull her back into his arms and kiss her some more.

It would be so easy to lift her lips to his again and forget about their weeks apart, about the problems keeping her from inviting him to stay with her in the attic. But he was right. Kissing didn't solve anything between them.

"Are you okay with this? Us kissing?" He grinned like he was proud of himself for gaining her approval. Or maybe for having kissed her like the husband he wished he'd been all along.

"I'm okay with it."

How could she say she wasn't okay with them kissing if she was the one who lunged into his arms? But she couldn't outright say if he'd kissed her as passionately every day over the past five years, she wouldn't be sleeping in the attic alone, either. And if he kept kissing her …

Her heart pounded even more erratically.

Peter clasped her right hand with his left, his gaze still tangling with hers, and led her back toward the project house. "Like I told you before, I'm not going anywhere until after the first of the year."

"Good to know." Really good.

He leaned toward her and brushed his mouth against her cheek. Wanting more of what they experienced a few minutes ago, she turned so their lips met. Several sweet kisses later, she sighed.

"Nice beach walk, huh?" He winked at her.

"Sure was." She couldn't remove the grin from her face.

Had they stepped into a magical world of misty rain falling all around them, and her and Peter kissing like a couple who were deeply, wildly in love with each other, then grinning like silly idiots? If so, what else might happen in their magical mist if only she let it transpire?

Three

"I thought you were keeping Mia Till away from the prisoner!" Forest clutched his cell phone tightly against his ear and paced across his and Paige's living room.

"You're the one who demanded she not be allowed to visit Edward." A slurping sound came through the speaker as if Deputy Brian was guzzling coffee. "He's been in Florence for nearly a month. What's the big deal about Mia visiting Evie?"

"What about possible collusion between the two?"

"No evidence of that."

Forest gritted his teeth. He was off the case and couldn't make demands of the deputy. However, he was still emotionally invested in the process. The fact he hadn't figured out how Mia previously communicated with Edward Grant, the lousy former mayor of Basalt Bay, burned inside him like salt dumped on a wound. What had he overlooked?

"Call Sheriff Morris if you want." Brian chuckled. "But after that journalist's scathing article in the newspaper, your word around here is sketchy at best."

Forest groaned. The article certainly took the wind out of his sails. Since it came out three weeks ago, he hadn't received a single request for his services as a private investigator. *Thanks a lot, A. Riley.*

Sheriff Morris demanded his silence too. He wasn't allowed to say anything about the article publicly. Not even to question the journalist about her source. That wasn't fair. Not when his career and integrity were on the line.

"How did you hear about Mia visiting Evie?" Deputy Brian asked.

"The local grapevine. Where else?"

No reason to mention it was Callie Cedars who told him about the "blond bombshell" who was spreading stories at Bert's that she supposedly heard from Evie.

"How is Evie getting information from Edward?" Forest would like the chance to question her. "Is it all Mia? I told you to keep an eye on her."

"Oh, I've got my eye on her." Brian cackled like he told a joke. "But since you're done with the task force, your advice is null and void."

The dig hurt. "Be careful. When this goes down and everything is exposed, you could be held responsible."

"I doubt that." Brian chortled. "If anyone's in the hot seat, it's you."

Acid burned up Forest's throat. "When do you expect Mia's next delivery of library books?"

"Later today. Why?"

"I'm still trying to figure some things out."

"You can't stir up the hornets and not expect to get stung," Brian said in a mocking tone.

"As an officer of the law—"

"That's right. I'm the officer of the law." Brian's voice rose. "You're in the private sector. Got it?"

"Loud and clear." Ending the call, Forest was tempted to hurl his phone at the wall. Not the reaction he wanted, but his frustrations were mounting.

With the trial to convict Edward of kidnapping and doing bodily harm to Paisley less than a month away, what if he'd missed something vital? What if Deputy Brian was overlooking something too?

Four

A pariah would have felt more welcome in Bert's Fish Shack than Craig Masters did wearing his fluorescent-green vest with "Basalt Bay Jail" written in black letters across the front and back. Nothing like announcing to the whole town he'd done some bad things and must repay his debt to society.

He'd told Detective Harper he would accept community service until the end of time. Apparently, Forest took him at his word. Five hundred hours felt like he'd be prying gum and cigarette butts from the streets and sidewalks of Basalt Bay for the rest of his life. Only two weeks since he started. Fifty hours down. Four-hundred fifty more to go. Yep, until the end of time.

The five-hundred-hour stint wasn't the only thing hanging over his head, either. Forest required two other stipulations of him—anger management classes and a lifetime pass to Alcoholics Anonymous. At least his permanent residence wasn't in the pokey.

Picturing his mom sitting in a jail cell tugged at his guilt levels. Evie brought her consequences on herself. But Craig felt remorse every time he imagined her being behind the same bars where he'd been incarcerated. And the fact he was free, or mostly free, while she was in jail burned at his conscience.

From the first table near the entrance to Bert's, he sat close enough to observe everyone who entered the diner. Near enough to observe Al Riley when she walked through the door. Although he half expected the journalist to ditch his invitation.

Upon entry, several people pegged him with a glare or a raised eyebrow as if questioning his presence in his pariah outfit. He tried to not make eye contact, just sipping his coffee and minding his own business. But each jangle of the bell meant the new customer might be Al, so he kept checking.

After the shakedown article she wrote about Forest a few weeks ago, she was nearly as much of a pariah in Basalt Bay as Craig was. The two of them having coffee together would probably create a scandalous wave of gossip. He almost grinned, imagining the locals yakking about them— *"That newspaper reporter is sullying her reputation even more by hanging out with the local riffraff."*

However, the strains of "White Christmas" filling the airwaves annoyed him and kept any humor at bay. He'd slept through Thanksgiving—better than giving in to the temptation to drink the day away. He ignored all the texts Judah sent inviting him for dinner. Texts from Forest? Those he was legally obligated to answer.

More recently, the texts from Judah inviting him to Christmas Eve dinner? Those he avoided like the plague. He didn't need "Jingle Bells" or "comfort and joy" or whatever sentimental holiday nonsense the Grant/Cedars families might indulge in. He couldn't stomach any more pretense. He wasn't really a part of their family. No doubt they hated the idea of him joining them for even one day of holiday cheer.

No, he'd stick to his community service regimen, try to find someone willing to hire an ex-con, and ignore the rest of the population of Basalt Bay until he put in every single hour of manual labor. Let the rest of the town enjoy their holiday festivities. He was out.

The doorbell jangled again. Maggie Thomas entered.

Craig groaned and averted his gaze. The opinionated battleax was exactly the type of person he didn't want to talk to. He hunched his shoulders, brooding over his coffee, hoping the innkeeper wouldn't notice him. How could anyone not notice him when he wore the neon vest labeling him a public offender?

"What do we have here?" Maggie gawked at him. "Why if it isn't the notorious bandit, Craig Masters! Aren't you supposed to be behind bars? How'd they let you escape?" Her peach pantsuit looked like a relic from a bygone era. Her thick-soled shoes tapped the floor double-time.

Glancing up, he met her condescending gaze, and a rush of irritation doused any polite response.

"Cat got your tongue?" She peered down at him as she might do to a naughty child. "I expect you'll be coming out to the inn. Cleaning my parking lot, hmm?"

"So the court order says," he said tightly.

"Sand removal should keep you sweeping my lot for a

year." Cackling, she stood to her full height. "Maybe some physical labor will teach you a lesson."

"What lesson might that be?" He shouldn't invite her ridicule, but the woman was getting under his skin. He wouldn't mind telling her where she could stuff her condescension and arrogance.

"You and your father are two peas in a pod." She rolled her eyes toward the ceiling. "Cut out of the same cloth. You both belong behind bars."

Nothing he hadn't thought of himself. But hearing the outspoken woman make the unwelcome comparison made him itch for a fight. "Listen here, you bag of wind, I'm not Edward Grant! You think he'd sit here and take this trash talk from you?"

Maggie gasped noisily like her tongue got caught in her throat.

"He'd wipe the floor with your snooty attitude and send you packing. Same as I should be doing."

"Why, I never." The woman's upper body swelled like a balloon about to pop. "Don't you dare speak to me that way! I've been a citizen of Basalt Bay my whole life. I demand respect!"

Respect. Right.

She thumped her knuckles against his table like a judge with a gavel. "I'm aware of your dark secrets, buster. I know what you did!"

Some of Craig's anger wilted into a pile of dead leaves. What did she know? Had everyone in the room heard about his attempts to follow Edward's plans? The stupid things he'd gone along with to try to buy the man's approval? Were they all judging him? He peered around the room, meeting a couple of stern gazes.

"Maggie!" Bert announced in his usual over-the-top manner as he stopped at the table. "Is everything all right over here?" He cast a wary eye at Craig.

"This … this reprobate called me a bag of wind." Maggie jabbed her finger toward him.

"Oh?" Bert twisted his handlebar mustache, drawing out the points. He might have been fighting a smile, too. "That right, Masters?"

"Peace and quiet are all I ask for while I finish my coffee. Is that too much to expect?"

"Not at all. Come along, Maggie. We have fresh apple pie. How about a piece on the house?" Bert led the cantankerous woman farther into the diner, discussing the breaded salmon on the menu.

Maggie Thomas, and others like her, were nothing but gossips bent on propagating lies and retelling stories that stretched the truth to absurd proportions. Small towns had their charm, but Craig couldn't wait to be done with his five hundred hours, making restitution where possible, his AA meetings, and then facing his backside to the sunset.

The door jangled. Al Riley—a grownup version of the girl he remembered from his brief stint in the Florence Elementary School during one of his mom's trips to Oregon—strode in wearing a forest green sweater dress and black heels. Not many in this town wore spikey heels like that, other than Mia Till. This blond possessed the perfect amount of highlights, making her hair sparkle as she walked. Tall and gorgeous, she filled out her sweater just right, too.

He met her gaze boldly. A gentleman would have stood and greeted her. Especially one who read trepidation in the woman's eyes the way he did. But he wore the dreadful vest. Didn't want to draw more attention to himself.

Al approached his table and sat down quickly, her head lowered as if not wanting to make eye contact with anyone, including him.

"Al."

Her gaze snapped up. "That wasn't cute when we were in fifth grade, and it isn't cute now."

Her blue eyes, the color of the sea on a beautiful day, blared at him. For ten seconds he felt dumbstruck. What a combination of beauty and fire!

"You don't like being called Al?"

"Never did. So cut it out." She picked up the menu Lucy Carmichael left on his table earlier. "Now, what's this about? Why'd you ask to see me?" She lifted her chin toward his vest. "Is this the dress code in Basalt Bay? You should have warned me to don appropriate apparel."

He snorted, relieved to find she still had the humor he recalled, despite her misplaced citified looks.

"I call it my pariah clothes."

"I can relate." Glancing around the room, she must have spotted Lucy. "Incoming at three o'clock."

Craig sat up straighter as Lucy swooped down on them, dusting her red hair back over her ears. "Alison, I'm surprised to find you here."

"Even a reporter has to eat." Al—because she'd always be that in Craig's mind—tapped her soft pink fingernail against the plastic-coated menu. "I'll have the Number Five."

.

"The Number—" Lucy sucked in air.

Craig stifled a laugh. The Number Five was big enough for two, maybe three. Al obviously didn't know that, and he wasn't about to tell her.

"What's so funny?"

"Nothing."

"What?" Al glanced between Craig and Lucy.

Craig took a long swallow of coffee, drowning another snicker.

"Coffee?" Lucy tucked one hand in her apron pocket.

"No, thanks. Water will suffice."

Lucy glanced at Craig. "What are you having?"

"I'll have the Number Two. I'm not as hungry as Al."

"Right." She winked at him and grabbed the menus before rushing off.

Al pelted him with a grim look. "I told you not to call me that. All I need is for locals to brand me as 'Al.'"

"It's Lucy. She probably remembers you from grade school."

"So? I'm a journalist. I'm all grown up."

"Is being a skulking editor for your uncle's newspaper your idea of a lifetime achievement?"

"I am not a skulking editor."

Her indignation was cute. But chitchat aside, he had questions for her. Then he'd get over to the courthouse where he was supposed to be spraying down the ex-mayor's old stomping grounds. The thought of stepping foot on City Hall property put a bad taste in his mouth.

"You didn't answer my question. Why did you ask to talk

with me?" She lifted one penciled eyebrow. "If I remember correctly, I never was at the top of your playlist."

True. But with the snazzy way she looked right now? The curves, the sexy blue eyes peering at him, the city vibe exuding from her pores, putting her on his playlist sounded just fine.

Five

Alison returned Craig's stare with a barely tolerant appraisal. Why did she agree to meet up with this blast from her past? His reaching out to her, saying he wanted to see her about an important matter, was too intriguing to ignore, especially considering she'd carried a mile-wide crush on him in elementary school.

Ever since she wrote about Forest Harper in the *Gazette*, and since she refused to write a retraction like some of the locals demanded of her, she'd received a plethora of disturbing calls and visits. While she told every other person she didn't have time for a sit-down or a meet-and-greet, for some reason, maybe insanity, she said yes to Craig.

It was strange how childhood fascinations could haunt a person for decades. The silly infatuation shouldn't be taking up any of her brain space. Yet, she still remembered the dark-haired boy. The way his almost-black eyes twinkled in her direction across the classroom. How the other girls called him "cute." Right now, her heart pounded a powerful beat in her chest as she gazed back at the man's sultry eyes appraising her with equal intensity.

Lucy whisked up to their table, setting two water glasses down with a clink. She didn't say anything this time, thankfully.

"Oh, she likes you," Craig said as the server bustled away.

His smile was still to die for. That's probably how he snagged women these days. He didn't wear a wedding band. Must not be married. Did his flirty gaze proclaim him available and interested in takers? Not that she was interested. Goodness, no.

"I have a question to ask you."

Of course, he did.

"About the article? Like I've told all the other callers, I'm not revealing my source. You won't pry it out of me, no matter your charms."

"Prying it out of you would be an interesting endeavor." His lips spread wide, showing a nice white-teeth smile.

So he wanted to flirt with her?

She smiled back at him. "What is it, then?"

"I wanted to see you and—" He cleared his throat like he was uncertain how to go on. "Judah Grant is my brother. Rather, half-brother." He lifted his chin. "Forest is his brother-in-law. Sort of all in the family."

"As in Mayor Grant's son?" She was still stuck on that tidbit. "You're—"

"Yep. His disappointing child." The smirk back on his face, all signs of emotional vulnerability vanished.

"Well, well. I hadn't heard that news."

"Me neither until about four weeks ago." He nodded

toward some other customers. "I'm surprised they didn't line up in front of the *Gazette* office to inform you."

"If you hadn't noticed, I'm not the most popular person in town. I've been getting troublesome texts, calls, and even threats." She took in a sharp breath. "People are demanding a retraction I won't give."

"Threats, huh?" His forehead puckered. "Where's your uncle? Shouldn't Milton be the one standing at the helm? Taking the flak?"

If only. She sipped her water, not wanting to discuss Uncle Milton's private affairs. "I wrote what I wrote. I have First Amendment rights."

"Sure you do." He leaned forward as if not wanting others to hear him. "But what if you wrote something false? Even libelous?"

How dare he accuse her of that! "Look, smart aleck, think what you will. It's a free country."

"Oh, I will think what I want."

The way his gaze wandered over her sent chills up her spine. She gritted her teeth so she wouldn't smile back at him this time. He had insulted her, hadn't he?

"This town can't sit on the truth for years without it never being exposed. The article about Forest was just the beginning. There's more to the story, so get ready."

"Everyone's dirty secrets uncovered? The truth in all its ugliness displayed across the front page?" His grin faded to a tight line. "Even if it hurts the innocent? What I don't understand is why you'd consider Mia Till a reliable source."

"Who says she's my source?" She kept her voice firm.

He squinted at her. "Why would you take the word of an insider for Edward Grant as truth?"

"What do you know about it?" Some of Ali's bluster melted in her seat, but she wouldn't show her hand. She stared at the frustratingly handsome man, tempted to walk out of the diner. But she was hungry. She wanted that breakfast.

"It was her, right?" Craig's dark brooding gaze pegged her. "I recognized the wording. Mia and I were coworkers ... let's say, friends ... for a while."

"You and her—?" Ali gulped. "I shouldn't be talking with you."

Pushing back from the table, despite her stomach growling in protest, she almost leaped up and marched to the door. Craig gently taking her hand in his sent sparks shooting through every vein and cell in her body. She should pull away, shouldn't let him touch her, yet she didn't move. Heat burned through the places where their fingers touched. Her gaze locked on his by an invisible cord spanning over twenty years and that ridiculous fifth-grade crush.

"I didn't say she and I were an item."

"No?" This time she did pull away.

He held up his hands, palms out. "Don't leave a fine breakfast on my account. Besides, I'm going to enjoy watching you eat it."

Lucy arrived and set down a plate piled obscenely high in front of Ali. She'd never seen such a mound of food for one person before. No wonder Lucy and Craig laughed at her.

Craig's mirth-filled eyes shimmered at her. His plate contained a fraction of the eggs and potatoes Ali's did.

"You must be awfully hungry today." Lucy rolled her eyes. "Same tab or separate?"

"Separate," Ali answered.

"Same," Craig said.

"I'll buy my own food, thank you."

"I always pay for dates I've arranged." Craig grinned rakishly at her.

"Oh, brother." Lucy stomped back toward the kitchen.

"This isn't a date," Ali said through clenched teeth.

"No, I don't suppose it is."

Despite her irritation with him, she stared longingly at the pile of hash browns, sausage, and cheese-covered eggs, her stomach growling. Who cared who paid for it?

"How about we call a truce while we eat?" Craig stuffed a bite of blueberry pancake in his mouth, somehow smirking around his chewing. "We can fight some more afterward."

"Fine." Even if she couldn't devour all this food, she was going to wolf down as much as she could and enjoy every bite.

Continue fighting with Craig? That was an enticing offer she couldn't ignore.

Six

Peter and Dad were spending the afternoon helping Paige with hauling paintings and boxes of various artwork from her car into the gallery. With each piece, they had to wait for her instructions about where to place it. Sometimes, adjusting the paintings took two or three attempts before she settled on the perfectly balanced spot. "Set this one on that easel." Then, "On second thought, move it over there. Or maybe—" Peter felt like a caddy waiting for a golfer to tell him which club to use.

Ever since he got to town three weeks ago, his time was filled with assisting Ruby in the project house, or else helping Paige here in the gallery. He couldn't believe how quickly the time had gone by. Only ten days until Christmas Eve? Good thing he already had Ruby's Christmas gift. He pictured the ruby necklace tucked in his backpack at Dad's house.

One thing still troubled him. What could he do to improve things in their marriage? Their beach walk this morning was great. The kissing? Crazy good. But how were they going to get over their past hurdles enough to move on with their lives together? More talking and clearing the air? A knot the size of Oregon grew in his throat and choked him every time he thought of having a knockdown drag-out conversation with her. But hadn't he promised himself to do just that, if necessary?

Groaning, he wiped his hands over his month-old beard.

"Deep thoughts, brother?" Paige patted his arm.

"You could say that."

"I won't keep you away from Ruby much longer." She grinned as if she knew his thoughts.

She probably wouldn't understand about him wishing he and Ruby could head north without an argument. Without him having to bear his feelings to her first. He needed those things like he needed a fishing hook stuck in his scalp!

No doubt Paige was thrilled to be having Christmas together as a family. Truth be told, he was glad about that too. A decade had passed since he last celebrated Christmas Eve with his sisters and Dad. Still, he wanted to return to the *Lily Forever*. Staying away from her for so long felt neglectful, even if he was paying someone to look after her.

At Paige's instruction, he set a painting of a seagull standing on an old-looking piling on a tall easel. He placed one of a sand dollar with a black background on a smaller table easel. "How's this?" He half expected her to tell him to move the painting again.

She stared intensely at the display, her index finger poised against her chin. "I like it. You're getting the hang of this, big bro."

"I doubt that." He never imagined himself doing art staging before. Not with his thick fingers and stocky physique.

Thank goodness he hadn't knocked anything valuable over yet.

"These are something," Dad commented from the other side of the room. "Come take a look."

Since Peter had moved into Dad's house, they were talking more. Not heavy discussions, by any means. But being around his father, helping with repairs and chores, prepping meals, even watching football together on Dad's old TV, they developed a rhythm of coexisting. Maybe even friendship. Although Peter figured Dad tiptoed around the past as much as he did.

"What's that?" Peter strode over to where his father arranged glass art on a folding table covered with a black cloth.

"I never saw anything like these before." Dad stared pensively at the display, swaying from side to side. "Watch how the glass catches the light when you move."

"Those are Kathleen's mosaics! You know the lady who co-owns the project house with Aunt Callie and Bess?" Paige called over. "They're so pretty, I'm tempted to buy all of them."

Peter shifted his feet back and forth. Sure enough, the light danced across the surfaces of the glass pieces. "I like this one." He pointed at a mosaic of a dory secured to a dock with a rope and the waves buffeting it.

Paige linked her arms with Dad's and Peter's. "It does my heart good to see you both interested in art. Thanks for the help, you guys. I couldn't have done all this without you." She let go of their arms and adjusted a couple of the mosaic pieces surrounded by distressed wooden frames

Peter almost laughed at her need for perfection, but he appreciated that about her too. He felt the same urgings with items on his boat. Everything had to be set up his way. Master and commander, he imagined Ruby calling him.

A conversation they had before she left came to mind. "Did you move the box of fishing hooks?" he'd asked. He always returned the box to its proper place in the outdoor bin of tools. Never left it out in the elements where the parts might get rusty or damaged.

"I put it in a different container, is all." She shrugged. "What does it matter if it's in one place or another?"

It mattered. Oh, it mattered!

So he understood why all these small adjustments to the art pieces mattered to Paige, too.

"Anything else we can do before we leave?" He tweaked a frame hanging unevenly on the wall.

"There are a couple more boxes of art to be displayed. If you want to give me a hand with those, I'd appreciate it."

"Will do."

Peter helped her set up a couple of displays from different artists. There was one of a beautiful shell on the seashore in watercolors. Another in bright oil colors of a racecar tearing down a country road. A vibrantly colored—

"Hey. What's this doing here?" He held up a familiar picture of an eye with swirls around it like the wind was guiding it.

"It's Mom's," Paige said almost reverently. "I reframed it."

"Yeah, but what's it doing here?" He didn't feel protective of it. But why was Paige selling off Mom's paintings? Was Dad okay with this? He glanced over his shoulder.

"What's troubling you, Pete?" Dad shuffled up to him.

"You okay with selling Mom's work?"

Dad shrugged. "Paige convinced me to try and see if anyone would buy it. Still lots of your mother's paintings in the pantry and in the attic, not to mention the ones on the walls. I'm okay with selling a few to someone who might enjoy them. More than you and I do, anyway."

Peter nodded at Paige. "Okay, then."

Considering Dad had been a widower for three years, maybe getting rid of some of Mom's paintings was a healthy stage for him. A good sign.

As Peter and Dad worked together, helping Paige get ready for her opening, it felt like something in their relationship shifted. Perhaps, Peter's sense of wrongs about the past altered or softened. Or maybe just being with his family was a healing balm he'd needed for a long time.

Seven

Hunched down in his car outside the deputy's office, Forest peered over the steering wheel, waiting for Mia to exit the building. Ever since he watched her scurry inside, everything within him wanted to charge in there and see what she was doing. Demand some answers.

Unfortunately, he was off the timeclock, so he had to rein in his detective instincts. Yet he was still pursuing justice and hoping to resolve his curiosity. If he discovered Mia's involvement with Edward had been criminal, the way she passed messages between the prisoner and townspeople, including some questionable threats, he'd report her actions to Sheriff Morris. Surely with enough evidence, the task force leader would pursue justice, even with the trial date closing in on them.

Mia had been in the deputy's office for exactly seventeen minutes and thirty-one seconds when the door opened. She sashayed toward her sports car with two books clutched to her chest. Library books? Was she transporting messages via books for Evie in the same way Forest thought she'd done in the past?

"What are you up to?" he muttered.

Mia slipped into her red car and zoomed off down the street. Forest sat up and started his car engine. Moving the vehicle forward, he maintained a block's distance between them.

Since Mia drove such a flashy car, it was easy to spot in front of the Post Office. Why did she go from the jail to the Post Office when she had library books to return?

Forest parallel parked three cars behind her vehicle. He shut off his engine and hunkered down in his seat again.

A few minutes later, Mia exited the Post Office, waving at a couple of people. Before entering her car, she glanced in Forest's direction. Did she recognize his car?

Groaning, he scooted lower. Any more and he'd be lying on his seat.

As soon as the red car pulled out, Forest started up his rig and followed Mia. Not far ahead, she pulled into a parking spot next to the library. He turned into the parking lot at Bert's where he'd have a good view of the library entrance without her seeing him. She strode inside just like he expected her to do.

He thought of the day he watched her getting library books, taking them to the prisoners, then returning books. Oh, wait. Something was different. This time she went to the Post Office before going to the library. Any chance Evie gave her mail to send to Edward? Had she previously delivered mail to Evie from Edward?

If so, what kind of plots might they be scheming? It

seemed like Mia was still involved with doing something devious for Edward. Or Evie. Those two were up to their ears in trouble! Why would Mia risk doing anything for either of them?

Eight

The front door creaked open to the one-room newspaper office, pulling Ali out of her trance-like staring at the computer screen. She'd spent the last hour researching public data about C-MER, trying to discover the cause of the dike delay. That was another hotbed piece Uncle Milton told her to tackle. So far, she hadn't discovered anything unusual.

A dark-haired woman wearing a soft pink sweater over blue jeans stepped into the office. She gazed around the cluttered space uncertainly.

"May I help you?" Ali asked without standing.

"I hope so." The woman walked around the counter piled high with old newspapers. "Hello. I'm Paige Harper."

Harper? Tensing up, Ali nodded toward the lone chair across from her. "I'm Alison Riley. How can I help you?"

"Nice to meet you." Paige dropped into the chair. "I've never been in the newspaper office before."

"It's not much to brag about."

The tentative look on Paige's face faded. "Can we talk?"

"Certainly."

"Would it be possible for me to write something for your paper, er, Milton's paper? He's your uncle, right?" Paige chuckled nervously. "I've never done something like this, and I'm curious what the steps might be."

"Yes, my uncle is the owner. Do you mean like an editorial?" Ali picked up a pen and tapped it against the desktop.

"Sounds right."

So this was Paige Harper, wife to Forest, and sister to Paisley, Edward Grant's daughter-in-law. Ali had done her homework by gathering information about some of the residents here.

"My husband can't comment about what I think was an unfair article, so I want to do so." She didn't sound angry. Just stating facts, although she was obviously emotional about it.

"This isn't a gossip column where everyone with a beef gets to air their complaints." Ali felt riled at the thought of anyone assuming she wrote gossip pieces.

"No?"

"No!" She tossed the pen on the desk.

"I'm sorry, but your article sounded like that to me. Your negative opinion against my husband was probably based on rumors."

"That is not the case. It was an honest article based on—"

"Someone's lies?"

Ali groaned. Twice in twenty-four hours someone had dumped on her source. Her uncle checked everything properly. Otherwise, he never would have given her the assignment.

"I'm sorry. That wasn't kind of me." Paige's smile looked forced. "I'm not trying to be mean. Forest is my husband of one whole month. However, I've known him for several years. He's a good man who believes in his work and helping people get justice."

"Paige, what you've said is biased."

"Yes, it is. I'd like the chance to stand up for him publicly."

"Paige—"

"What would be wrong with me writing my opinion in the paper after your bold, harsh statements against him and his career choices?"

Heat flooded up Ali's neck. Her face must be maroon by now. She despised the way her cheeks gave away her anger, doubts, jealousy, or whatever fickle emotion hit her.

"Or what if you wrote a retraction?" Paige asked in a softer tone of voice. "Newspaper writers do that sometimes, right?"

"If she was absolutely wrong about her facts." Ali thrust her hands in the air. "That isn't the case here. Look, I can't give you carte blanche about an editorial. But nothing's stopping you from writing a letter to the editor."

"You won't accept an opinion piece?"

"Do you realize the phone calls I've received since I wrote the article? The disgruntled readership?"

Paige shook her head.

"I can hardly walk down the sidewalk without someone throwing proverbial tomatoes at me."

"I'm sorry. I didn't like the residents of my hometown whispering about me, either." Paige sighed. "However, since it's the Christmas season, I thought you might be willing to bring some peace and unity to our town. There's been enough strife." She stood and strolled toward a picture on the wall as if drawn to it.

"It isn't my job to bring peace." Ali wanted to set the record straight. "It's my task to pursue the truth and reveal it."

"Truth as you see it, right?" Paige met Ali's gaze, a challenge in her eyes. "This is lovely." She nodded toward the ink drawing of a ship at sea in a storm.

"My mother did it when I was small."

"Do you have more? I'm opening the art gallery, and I'd love to have some prints like this to show."

"Sorry. I don't have any others." Looking at the picture brought sadness to Ali's heart. "Flood damage after Addy and Blaine destroyed most of the stored items."

"I'm sorry. This is really beautiful." Paige moved toward the door. "I'll consider writing a letter to the editor. You'll publish it if I write one?"

"Sure. Why not?" Although, if her writing was too biased, Ali would have to edit it. "All submissions are subject to vetting and an editorial process."

"I would hope so."

Her parting comment hit Ali between the eyes. Paige meant her. Like she hoped Ali vetted her source. Uncle Milton had done that, right?

Nine

Paige went from the *Gazette* office directly to the project house. Now she stood in front of the large dining room window, waiting for Aunt Callie to prepare their tea. If anyone could help her come up with a plan, her aunt could.

One measly letter to the editor wouldn't make much of a statement. But what if the small-town press was inundated with letters to the editor?

"Here we are." Aunt Callie bustled into the room carrying a tray with two teacups and a small plate of cookies.

"Looks lovely. Thank you."

They sat down at the wooden dining table Aunt Callie, Bess, and Kathleen had picked out before Thanksgiving.

"Now, what's this about? You look like you have something up your sleeve." Aunt Callie took a bite of a shortbread cookie with jam on top. "Try these. Kathleen made them last night."

Paige picked up a cookie. "Are you ladies enjoying your new kitchen?" She bit into the soft, delicious sweetness. "Mmm. These are wonderful."

"Yes, we are. After our successful Thanksgiving dinner, we can't wait to celebrate Christmas Eve here, too. You will come, won't you? You and Piper, and"—Aunt Callie cleared her throat as if choking on cookie crumbs—"your husband?"

"Certainly. Forest's family will be here, also."

"That's right. I almost forgot." Aunt Callie sipped her tea. "Do they need a place to stay?"

"No. They've booked rooms at the Beachside Inn." Paige toyed with the edge of her cookie against her saucer. "There will be five of them—Forest's mom and dad, his sister, and two nephews. Four-year-old twins."

"And the sister's husband?"

"Separated, I'm afraid."

"I see," Aunt Callie said in one of those tones she used when she didn't like something.

Paige didn't plan to discuss Forest's family with her aunt. They had enough problems in their own family without dishing out advice or judgment on anyone else's.

"I want to talk with you about the newspaper article from a few weeks ago."

"I thought you put that behind you."

"Temporarily, yes." Paige nibbled on her cookie. "The way Alison Riley put such harsh criticisms of Forest in everyone's thoughts still bugs me."

"He wasn't a beloved member of our community before that." Aunt Callie snorted.

"After she lambasted him, he didn't stand a chance." She let her emotions come out in her words. "That isn't right. I don't want her treated meanly, but I want her to face what she's done."

"Have you talked with Milton?"

"No. Just his niece. I was hoping she'd write a correction or an apology." Paige shrugged.

"And?"

"She's adamant she's right."

"Must run in the family." Aunt Callie grumbled. "Milton's a stubborn man, too. So, what do you have in mind?"

"According to Alison, she's already gotten some flak from readers. I'd like a landslide of letters to fall on her desk. Soon, if possible." While it might sound humorous, she was serious. "A. Riley needs to know people in Basalt Bay care about each other. We don't want our friends and family dumped on in the *Gazette!*"

"A deluge of Christmas revenge, huh?" Aunt Callie chuckled.

"Not revenge." Paige swallowed hard. Was setting the record straight for her husband wrong? Wasn't standing up for him a way of showing him her loving support? "More like an eye-opener."

"Hmm." Aunt Callie rested her fist against her chin, tapping her index finger next to her nose. "I will gladly spread the word encouraging a letter dump on our visiting journalist's desk. However, I don't have to stick up for that husband of yours, do I?"

"Aunt Callie—"

"I'll admit at Thanksgiving you two seemed … in love."

"We are in love."

"I still don't like the way he married you on the sly."

"I know." Maybe asking Aunt Callie to do this letter barrage was a mistake. "If you can't stand up for Forest, maybe you shouldn't be the one talking to the town about writing letters on his behalf. Forget I said anything."

Aunt Callie slurped her tea. "Are you still planning a wedding ceremony I can attend?"

"Yes. We haven't discussed it since Thanksgiving." She didn't mention Forest wanted to have a ceremony while his family was in town for Christmas. But she'd argued it would be a lot of pressure on her with the gallery opening too. "Probably in the new year."

Aunt Callie groaned. "Don't put it off too long."

"I won't."

"So, what do you want these letters to say?"

"Are you sure you want to help?"

"Of course. I'll call Maggie and Patty and start a message relay." Aunt Callie chuckled. "By tomorrow's mail delivery, A. Riley won't know what hit her."

"Okay. This is what I was thinking—"

Ten

Leaning over, Paisley hugged Judah where he sat working at his computer. "Any luck?"

"No interviews yet." He kissed her cheek. "Mmm. You smell nice."

"Thanks. Just showered." She had to get to work at the diner soon, but something was on her mind. So far, her idea was only a possibility. But wishes and daydreams had been playing through her thoughts. What if she was pregnant? What if she could tell Judah the good news as part of his Christmas present?

Should she mention her monthly cycle was a week late? Or should she keep her news to herself until she was certain? She didn't want to get his hopes up, only to be dashed. Still, she was eager to share even the possibility of a baby with him.

The last six weeks of them being together as husband and wife had been ideal. She felt loved and cherished, precious to him. And he to her. She'd married the best man in the world, twice! He'd make a great dad, too.

"You okay?"

"More than okay." She kissed the top of his head. "I have something to ask you."

"All right." He set down his laptop and stood. Linking their pinkies, he faced her. "What's up, sweetheart? Other than you smelling nice and being cuddly?" He grinned at her in the way she loved.

She smiled back at him. "What do you have left to do on the project house?"

"Just outside tasks, weather permitting. The roof's done. Ruby's almost finished with the attic. We'll build the back deck in the spring. Why do you ask?"

"I have a project for you to do if you're willing." She adjusted her hands to clasp his more firmly. "A Christmas gift to me, and to the community."

"Oh? What's that?"

"Remember how Forest mentioned having a vow renewal ceremony while his family is here for Christmas?"

"Yeah."

"How would you feel about the two of you building the gazebo out at Baker's Point before then?"

"Before—? I see where you're going with this." He skimmed the pads of his thumbs across her cheeks. "Does Paige want the ceremony to be out there?"

"No. I thought it might be a nice Christmas surprise for her." Paisley might have a secret to tell Judah there, if he built it, too. "Would you mind building the gazebo?" She stepped into his arms and leaned her cheek against his chest. "I'd love to have the place where you proposed to me the first time back up again."

She felt his heart beating strongly beneath her ear. Smelled the Old Spice scent of his deodorant and soap. Warm thoughts of lying in his arms flooded her brain. Too bad she had to leave for work soon.

Why wasn't he answering her? She met his gaze. "Are you too busy this week? I don't mean to pressure you."

"I had hoped to keep job hunting today. I have to land a steady position soon."

"It doesn't have to be today." She ran her palms over his arms. *We might be having a baby.* She wanted to shout the good news to him. She clenched her teeth together to stop herself from saying the words burning in her thoughts. "You and Forest could build the structure in an afternoon or so, couldn't you?"

"You think I'm superhuman?" His mouth twitched.

"Sometimes." His lips were too tempting not to kiss again. Warmth spread through her as she moved her mouth over his, loving how he pulled her against him and kissed her back, long and sweet. "So, you'll do it?"

"I'll do anything for you," he murmured.

Their lips met again. Fire meeting fire.

She might get to Bert's a little bit later than usual, but she couldn't resist spending more romantic time with her husband.

Eleven

Forest handed Piper a sippy cup with juice in it. "Stay here in the kitchen with that, okay, princess?"

"Mmm." Piper sipped from the cup.

"I don't want you spilling anything on the rug. Your mama will wring my neck."

"Mmm." She bobbed her head up and down.

Mulling over the conversation he needed to have with the deputy, Forest strode into the living room. He paused to admire Paige's framed paintings that were all lined up on the carpet, leaning against the couch and chair. The pieces appeared ready for transport to the gallery. What a fabulous collection she'd created! He loved her artwork.

Paige scurried into the room carrying a couple of small-framed pictures. "This should do it. Twelve in all." The pictures in her hands were of the peninsula near City Beach.

"They're amazing. I'm so proud of you."

"Yeah?" Her eyes sparkled up at him.

He planted a kiss on her lips. "I'm one lucky guy for convincing you to marry me."

"Hmm. You're not trying to get out of helping me haul all of these paintings out to the car, are you?"

"Not on your life." He flexed his arm muscles. "I'm ready to do whatever you need me to do."

"Good." She squeezed his bicep and grinned. "Can you grab the stack of blankets and plastic wrap off the bed? We'll have to protect each piece before taking them outside."

"Sure thing." He jogged back to the bedroom and scooped up the bedding.

"Piper! Nooooo!"

Forest froze at the shocked tone in Paige's voice. What in the world? He sprinted back to the living room.

Oh, no. Oh, no.

Paige stood motionless, her pained expression aimed at her biggest painting of the lighthouse that now had red liquid dripping down its surface. Forest felt her anguish go right through him. His gaze leaped to Piper who was squatting in front of the painting, grinning like she'd done a fabulous thing. Her upside-down sippy cup was still in her hand.

"Paige. I'm so sorry."

"I can't believe this!" She dashed into the kitchen.

This was all his fault. Forest dropped the pile of blankets on the couch. Then picked up Piper. He was the one who handed the two-year-old the cup and told her to stay in the kitchen. But then, he got distracted with the paintings, and with kissing Paige. Not focusing on what Piper might do with the cup.

Paige stormed back into the room with a roll of paper towels and a wad of damp ones. "I didn't know she had her cup."

"That was my fault. I'm sorry."

"*Mow. Mow.*" Piper bounced the cup off his shoulders.

"You've had quite enough, young lady!" Paige flicked a glare in Forest's direction. She knelt by the painting, dabbing the canvas gently, lovingly.

Forest swallowed a behemoth gulp. "Is it going to be okay?"

"I don't know." She patted at the red juice with the paper towel. "This was supposed to be my centerpiece for the gallery. How did this happen?"

"I gave Piper—" He groaned. "Doesn't matter."

"Mommy." Piper reached her hands toward Paige.

"Mommy's busy."

"Mommy!"

Forest jostled Piper and strode into the kitchen, hoping to distract her from a tantrum. "Remember you were supposed to stay in here with the cup?"

"Mmm." Piper smiled, oblivious to the trouble she'd caused.

No use crying over spilled milk, or in this case, spilled juice. But Paige's masterpiece pockmarked with red, her shocked expression, and her glare aimed right at him, were heartbreaking.

Wadding up red-stained paper towels, Paige marched across the room to the garbage can. "It'll take some touching up, but I got to it quickly, so I think it'll be all right."

"That's good news."

She nodded but didn't meet his gaze.

"I told her to stay in the kitchen." What else could he say? He was new to this fathering business, but that was no excuse. He should have paid closer attention to Piper.

Paige heaved a sigh. "She's two. Doesn't listen to instructions well."

"I am sorry."

"It isn't your fault."

Maybe she wasn't exactly mad at him. Just disappointed.

"What can I do to help?" He set Piper down. "Still want me to load up those paintings?"

"Yes, thanks. Each piece must be wrapped and placed 'carefully' in the car." She nodded toward the living room. "If you wouldn't mind helping with that, I'll grab Piper's backpack and take her over to Necia's."

"Absolutely."

Paige scooped up Piper and hurried down the hallway.

Forest sighed. How quickly things flipped emotionally in his and Paige's relationship. Moments ago, he was kissing her. She was acting warm and flirty. Then he stepped out of the room. Bam! Everything changed.

Accidents happened. Paige was understandably upset about her art piece getting damaged. Maybe frustrated with him for not watching Piper better. But still. When would they find stable footing?

As meticulously as possible, he wrapped each of the frames and transported them to Paige's car, hoping her gallery opening ran smoother than this morning had started.

Twelve

An hour later, after helping Paige unload her paintings at the gallery, Forest strode into Deputy Brian's office.

The lawman glanced up from his computer, a frown on his face. "What are you doing here?"

"We need to talk." Forest dragged a straight-back chair over to the corner of Brian's desk, then sat down. "I need your help."

"How so?"

Forest decided to set aside his hurt pride and appeal to the deputy's sense of loyalty and service to the town. "You care about Basalt Bay, right? You're trying to do a good job for the community. A great job, even."

"Sure, sure."

"You want Edward and Evie to face the consequences for their actions, true?"

"What's this got to do with anything?"

"A piece of Edward's case data, or the lack thereof, still bothers me. I've lost sleep over it, too." Forest leaned his arms against the edge of the desk. "What would you say about working on solving it with me?"

"Solving it?" Brian rolled his eyes. "Is this about Mia?"

"Yes, it is. She's bringing books to Evie, then returning them to the library, correct?"

"Yeah. So what?" Brian huffed out a breath.

"I still think she's doing something underhanded."

"Come on, man." Brian fist-bumped the surface of the desk. "You went through every one of those books when Edward was here and didn't find a thing! Made a fool of yourself in the process. Now you want to do the same thing again?"

"Not quite." Forest called on every bit of willpower he possessed not to stand up for himself and walk out of the office. Instead, he tried to keep his voice humble, his heart humble, too. "What if I missed something? What if I made a big mistake?"

"What kind of mistake?" Brian peered at him suspiciously.

"What if the messages Mia passed from Edward didn't have anything to do with the library books?"

"That's what I figured all along." Brian thrust out his hands.

"Exactly. So, maybe, you wouldn't mind doing me a favor."

"Such as?"

"Would you call one of your buddies down at the Florence precinct and ask if Edward has received any mail this week?"

"What does that matter?" Brian asked gruffly. "They'd check it anyway."

"Of course, they would." Forest smoothed his palms together. "Just call the officer in charge and find out if

Edward got any mail from Basalt Bay this week, okay? Namely, from Evie or Mia."

"Evie didn't send any mail out. I've been watching her like a hawk." Brian crossed his arms over the cluttered surface of the desk. "Kept my eye on Mia while she was here, too."

"I'm sure you're doing a fine job." Again, Forest kept his voice light. "Evie didn't ask you to mail anything, did she?"

"Nope. Oh. Are you saying Mia did that?"

"Possibly. She went to the Post Office immediately after leaving here two days ago."

"How do you know that?"

"I followed her."

Brian groaned. "It still doesn't prove—"

"But it might. Will you help me figure it out? That's all I'm asking."

"This is a waste of time. A waste of the taxpayers' money." Brian eyed Forest for about fifteen seconds. Then he snatched up the telephone from the desk and thumbed in the number. Clutching the device to his ear, he said, "This is Deputy Brian in Basalt Bay. Can you check if Edward Grant received any mail from here recently?" A silence. "Yes, I know the ban's been lifted. Just answer the question, will you?" A pause. "Thanks. I owe you."

He hung up. "Edward received two pieces of mail. One from Jenn Blanchard." He tipped his head toward the jail cell where Evie Masters was. "The other from—"

"Mia Till."

"Yep."

Just like he thought.

"It's not a crime for her to write to our ex-mayor," Brian said tightly.

"No. But it answers my question about how she may have been interacting with him before." Forest linked his fingers together and hooked them over his crossed knees. "That day I searched through the library books? You know, when I didn't find anything? My mistake was in not searching Mia."

"What?"

"She may have already taken a note out of the book before I spoke to her and hid it in her clothes."

"Right under my nose?"

"Perhaps." Forest didn't want to make him feel worse, but he still hoped for the man's assistance. "What do you think about setting up another sting?"

"Are you crazy?"

"Maybe." He grinned. "Let's find out how Mia was passing messages to and from Edward."

"The no-contact ban is lifted."

"I know." Forest stood and returned the chair to its spot. "But how involved was she, not only during the communication ban, but during the kidnapping?"

"You still think she was involved with that?" Brian shook his head.

"Shouldn't we do our due diligence and find out?" Forest tried to appeal to the lawman's sense of duty. "Like you said, I'm off the clock. You're the officer here. Messages traveled to and from Edward from this jail. Basalt Bay citizens were threatened. How did that happen on your watch?"

Brian stared at the ceiling. "Mia's a friend. I don't boast many of those. I'd hate to cause her needless trouble."

Forest gritted his teeth and zipped up his coat. "If you don't want to do this, I'll buzz Sheriff Morris. If he says to back off, I will. But I may have to explain that you let Mia bring library books to and from the prisoners without examining the books or searching her."

Brian groaned. "Just tell me your plan and get it over with."

Thirteen

Craig sprayed the power washer against the library's brick siding, and a blast of water ricocheted off the building, hitting him full in the face. Spitting and sputtering, he let go of the hose and it thudded onto the cement. He wiped his coat sleeve across his face. When he could finally see, Al was walking down the sidewalk straight toward him.

Her hands tucked into her trench-coat pockets, her slim form swayed back and forth, and she wore those tall heels that made her legs look like they went on and on forever.

He gulped and shut off the water spray. "Morning."

"Good morning." She chuckled and looked him over, probably seeing all the water splatters he was doused in. "I thought you slipped out of town. Maybe made a run for Mexico?"

He liked her smiling and bantering with him.

"Not quite. Are you off to decimate some poor soul?" He could give as good as she did.

"Ha." She stuffed her hands deeper into her pockets. "You have me pegged. Can't wait to do exactly that."

He grinned. Something about this woman brought out the humor in him. Made him feel lighthearted. More alive.

"How's the criminal reconciliation program going for you?" She lifted her chin toward the library.

"Off the record?" He stuffed his hands into his jacket pockets to warm them.

"Nothing for me to write about here, is there?"

"Nope. My life is one boring slate."

"I doubt that."

She lifted one eyebrow, making his pulse hammer. He wouldn't mind making her eyebrow quirk in surprise with something like a kiss. Or maybe throwing her in the bay. Whichever came first.

"Something amusing to you, Mr. Masters? What pray tell is your snarky expression for this time?"

"Just picturing myself tossing you over my shoulder and throwing you in the sea."

Her jaw dropped.

Perfect. She was speechless.

"Either you're flirting with me, or else you are a dangerous criminal." She chuckled. "Maybe you're the one I should be interviewing today."

He burst out a gut laugh. "You, Al Riley, take my breath away with your honesty and charm."

"Charm? Few would label me with that!"

A wide smile crossed those lips he couldn't stop staring at. Suddenly, his laughter evaporated, making his statement self-fulfilling. His breath was stolen away by her beauty. By her alluring smile that mocked him or said she was game for her breath being taken away—a heady thought.

"About an interview?" She pulled her hands out of her pockets and smoothed back a few strands of flyaway hair. Something he wouldn't mind doing for her.

What was he thinking? He was in the criminal reconciliation program. He had committed crimes worthy of jail time. His biological parents were both headed for prison. He had no right to be flirting with this woman. He picked up the power washer again and turned it on full blast.

"Excuse me," she shouted above the noise of the tool's motor. "Did I steal your thunder?"

Indeed, she had. But not for the reason she thought. Despite his thoughts on how incompatible they were, she was someone he wouldn't mind getting to know better. What would she say if he asked her out on a date?

Could his heart handle the rejection if she told him to jump into the sea?

Fourteen

Paige swept the entryway to the gallery, still frustrated over not being able to showcase her best art piece today. This event was only a soft opening, but she wanted everything to be in its rightful place, meaning her lighthouse painting should take center stage. A finished picture getting damaged had never happened to her before. She was so careful with her artwork. With everyone else's, too. In her line of work, she had to be!

A dark-haired woman, maybe in her late thirties, wearing grungy clothes and with a bulging hiker's backpack on her shoulders, paused outside the gallery, peering in the window. For just a second, something about her looked familiar.

"Good morning," Paige said.

"Hey." The woman gave her a distant look.

"Can I help you?"

"Nah."

A couple of weeks ago, Paige would have been more cautious about speaking to a stranger. Since Evie Masters was the one behind the threats toward her, and since she was in jail awaiting her trial, Paige felt more relaxed talking with people she didn't know. Not expecting others to have ulterior motives toward her made her feel safer.

Casting a long look through the window, the woman shuffled down the street, a slump to her shoulders. That pack must be awfully heavy. Was she homeless?

"Have a nice day," Paige called.

The woman didn't answer.

Compassion seeped into Paige's heart. *Lord, You know that woman's needs. Please touch her. Provide for her.*

Remembering how humbly Forest apologized about the juice being spilled on her painting, and how she left the house without assuring him things were okay between them, she added, *I'm sorry for overreacting this morning. Bless Forest. Thank You for my sweet family.*

She continued sweeping, contemplating her day.

Thanks to Bess's office making the arrangement, Alison was scheduled to drop by this morning to take Paige's picture for the newspaper. Apprehension was already building in her over having to speak with the journalist so soon after their letter-writing discussion yesterday. Had Aunt Callie spoken to any of her friends about flooding the newspaper office with letters supporting Forest yet? Had Paige done the right thing by requesting her aunt's help?

The click of heels preceded Alison's voice. "Paige? Is this a good time to get that picture?"

"Sure. Let me put this broom away." Setting the wooden-handled broom inside the building, she said another quick prayer. *Lord, help me to be gracious to her.*

"Right beneath your sign ought to be good." Alison waved toward the distressed wooden sign proclaiming, "Paige's Art Gallery & Coffee Shop."

The newspaper reporter seemed all business, not cracking a smile, no warm tones evident in her voice. She snapped a couple of pictures. Too bad she didn't take time to focus or adjust anything. That was the problem with camera phones. All the tweaking and personal touches of F-stop manipulation were lost.

"Mind if I peek inside? I might find a good shot in there."

"Of course. Come in."

Alison took a couple of pictures of the coffee shop. She glanced around at the art displays and said, "Hmm," a few times. "This should do."

"Thanks for putting the opening in the paper. I really appreciate it."

"Sure. Part of small-town charm, right?"

Paige tensed at her disapproving tone. Maybe Alison should go back to her big-city newspaper where she didn't have to be bothered with incidentals like a tiny gallery opening. Then her recent prayer about grace came to mind. Alison needed God's love and mercy like everyone did. Just like Paige did.

"Maybe you'd like to stop in and shop sometime?" she asked in what she hoped was a pleasant tone. "We have lots of artists' work represented. New things will be rotating weekly."

"Perhaps. When is your grand opening?" Alison tapped her phone like she was setting up a reminder.

Paige, Forest, and Bess had agreed to postpone the event until after the new year. Forest said he needed more time to make sure Evie's threat was no longer a possibility. Paige didn't see why he was so worried. With Edward and Evie in jail, weren't they finished with those concerns?

"In January, most likely. I don't have a date set."

"Let me know. If I'm still here, I'll try to fit the notification in the paper. Thanks." Alison exited the shop quickly.

Paige released a long sigh, letting go of some tension. Then she did a check of all the art pieces in the gallery, making sure everything was displayed properly.

At ten o'clock, she flipped the Closed sign hanging in front of the street-side window to Open for the first time since Hurricane Addy hit. So much good had brought her to this moment of reopening the gallery. So much generosity by others—Bess, Forest, Dad, Peter, and many members in the community who'd donated hours to helping her.

Bess Grant was the first customer through the doorway. "You did it, Paige!"

"We did it together."

Bess enveloped her in a hug. "I'm so proud of you."

"Thank you."

Her own mother saying those words wouldn't have pleased her more than hearing the mayor, her business partner, Paisley's mother-in-law, and Paige's friend, praise her.

"I've waited a long time for this."

"Me too." Bess strode toward the softly lit area on the far side of the coffee shop where Paige had arranged her own collection of paintings. "These are so lovely. All set for business?"

"Absolutely."

"Then I'll take this one." She pointed at a painting of Mountain Peak Rock. "This monolith is my favorite of all the rocks along the Pacific."

Excitement pulsed through Paige. Someone wanted to buy one of her paintings! She felt like dancing a few steps. Maybe squealing with glee. "Thank you, Bess. This means a lot to me."

"This will go in my office at City Hall." She gave Paige a meaningful look. "Everyone who meets with me will get a glimpse of your artwork. I'll tell them who the artist is—our own Paige Harper—and where they can purchase other paintings by local artists."

"I will gladly take all the publicity I can get."

"Good." Bess pulled her wallet out of her purse.

"But you've done so much for me already." Paige touched Bess's shoulder. "Why don't you take this as a gift from me?"

"None of that. I'm going to be a regular customer here." Bess swayed her hand toward the painting. "I'll pay full price for this treasure. Save it for me, will you? My assistant, Samantha, will pick it up later."

"Will do. Thank you so much." Paige made the financial transaction, wishing she could have done something nice for Bess, too.

"The project house needs some artwork, so I'll be back." Bess waved and strode toward the door. "Have a successful first day!"

"I hope so! Thank you."

The project house needed artwork, huh? Maybe Paige could help with that.

Fifteen

Forest had one official job assignment left on his docket. Overseeing Craig's community service detail wasn't how he'd choose to spend his morning, but that's why he was at Bert's. The place hummed with chatter and the occasional burst of laughter. Where was Craig? Obviously late.

"Detective"—Lucy topped off his cup—"didn't you say someone was meeting you?"

"That's right. He'll be along shortly."

Lucy smoothed her free hand over her long braid, smiling, not moving on to the next table as quickly as he would have liked. "I was sorry to read about you in the *Gazette*. Those things Al said weren't very nice. But who'd believe her anyway?"

"Al?"

"Alison Riley. What's with her vendetta against you? It's not like she knows anything about Basalt Bay." She chuckled. "Of course, you're new to town also. Swept Paige off her feet in two blinks."

The doorbell jangled. Craig strode toward Forest's table.

"Oh, Craig," Lucy gushed, "it's good to see you. Want some coffee?"

"That would be great. Thanks."

He dropped into the seat across from Forest, not mentioning his tardiness. Hopefully, he wasn't showing up late to all his community service duties.

"Hello, Craig."

"Hey." He slouched into the booth seat.

"Things going okay with your community service? Any problems?"

"You mean have I picked up enough trash to last a lifetime? If so, yes, sir."

Lucy dropped a cup on the table and filled it nearly to the brim. "You need anything else?" She raised an eyebrow toward Craig, sliding her tongue over her lower lip in a blatant invitation.

Craig's face reddened. "This is good. Thanks, Luce."

"If anything comes to mind, give a holler." Giggling, she sauntered off.

"Still charming the ladies, I see," Forest said.

"Why not?" Craig pointed at his vest. "Any woman who can look past this is worth charming."

Forest sipped his hot drink, then changed the subject. "Did you get the library finished?"

"Yep," Craig said testily.

"Have you started at the Beachside Inn?"

"Would be there now if it wasn't for this." Craig lifted his coffee cup. "Anything else, Detective? Want to know what I ate for dinner last night? If I can find a real job?"

At least something brought out strong emotion in Craig. Otherwise, his smirky, smart-alecky attitude seemed to be an armor he proudly wore.

"Look, this isn't easy for me either," Forest said.

"No?"

"You boys doing okay?" Lucy pranced up to their table. "We have fresh apple pie."

"We're fine, Luce."

"No problem." She eyed them and continued to the next table.

"You were saying? Checking in with me is tough on you? Why isn't Deputy Brian doing it, then? You'd be free to do whatever ex-detectives do."

Forest ground his teeth. Should he remind Craig that he took a chance on his plan to capture Evie? That he allowed his family to be put at risk so Craig could prove his innocence?

Instead, he asked, "How are the AA meetings going?"

"As well as you might imagine. Want to ask about my anger management classes too? Those are a hoot." Craig's taut face and clenched fists demonstrated he probably needed more of those classes.

"I'm glad to hear the meetings are ... helpful."

Craig snorted.

The bell jangled again. Red-faced, Alison stomped straight toward them, about twenty envelopes clutched between her hands. "Who's responsible for this bombardment of mail? You?" She glared at Forest. Her glare swung toward Craig. "How could you do this to me?"

"Al—"

"Don't 'Al' me."

"What are you talking about?" Craig scooted back, pulsing his hand toward the stack of envelopes. "What is this?"

"Like you don't know." Her intense glare raked over Forest. "Are you and your wife proud of yourselves? Turning the whole town against me?"

She held out the envelopes to him. There wasn't a return address in the top left corner. Anonymous mail?

"I have no idea what you're talking about. You wrote that article about me."

"So I did." She swiveled to Craig. "Is this your idea of a Merry Christmas? If so, thanks a lot!" Throwing a disparaging glance at Craig, then Forest, she traipsed out of the diner as forcefully as she'd entered.

"What was that about?" Forest asked.

"No idea. I've got to—" Craig leaped up. "Can this wait?"

"Sure, sure. Go." Forest waved, shooing him toward the door.

Stymied as to what just transpired, he dragged his wallet from his back pocket and threw a twenty on the table. Why did Alison assume he and Paige were involved with those letters?

Sixteen

Ali marched down the sidewalk, not making eye contact with anyone. Why had she stomped into the diner and accused Forest and Craig of manipulating letter writers without proof? Idiot.

Her head might have been turned by Craig since she returned to Basalt Bay. But this? Him, or Forest and Paige, instigating people to write hate mail? Why would Craig do that? How could he do that to her?

And anonymously written? Why weren't the letter writers brave enough to say who they were? Oh, this infuriated her.

Footsteps pounded behind her. She tensed. Walking faster, she didn't glance back. Some of the writers had sounded dangerous. Too bad she wasn't carrying any pepper spray.

"Al!"

Craig. She huffed out a breath. Not someone out to get her. Or was he—

"Al—"

Why did he continue to call her that ridiculous nickname when she told him not to? Reaching the newspaper office, she yanked her key out of her deep pocket.

"Thanks for stopping." Craig strode up to her and leaned his shoulder against the building beside her, their shoulders nearly touching.

She met his gaze for an instant, anger still pulsating through her veins. "What do you want? And stop calling me Al!"

He smiled. Infuriating man!

"Why'd you steamroll us in the diner? Who wrote those letters you're all fired up about?" He nodded at the pile of mail she still clutched.

"Why do you care?" She squinted at him, some of her irritation still frothing through her. She'd just about had enough of this town! Maybe of this man.

"I don't know, but I do," he said in a gentler tone. "You come charging into the diner, both guns blazing, then you don't even give Harper or me a chance to defend ourselves?"

"Just something else you don't understand about me." The lock gave way and she pushed open the door. Would have slammed it behind her if half of Craig's body wasn't blocking the doorframe. "Did you write any of these?" She had to know before allowing him into the office. She thrust the stack of envelopes under his nose, nearly smacking his chin.

"Not one. Why would I?"

She stared hard into his eyes for several seconds, trying to see into his conscience, if he had one. He met her gaze, blink for blink. In another setting, in another mood, that intensity and closeness, her peering into his deep blackish eyes, might have elicited a kiss.

Some of her stupid rage dripped out of her like blood from a cut. That's what she had, right? Wounded pride. A gaping sore of resentment toward this town. Toward anyone who might have pressured her uncle into withholding the truth, because it couldn't be his fault.

"Do you want to tell me what this is about?" Craig's soft voice strummed over her like a love song.

"Not really." Heat flooded her face. "I'd rather forget I made a spectacle of myself."

His chuckle sent vibrating shivers up her spine. Crazy reaction. What was she? In elementary school? Next, she'd be wanting to exchange dollar-store rings with him.

"You going to invite me in?"

"No." A smile creased her lips.

She didn't object when Craig followed her into the cluttered domain lacking any decorating sense. If this were her permanent office, she'd gut the place and transform it into a modern business.

"You don't take no for an answer very well, do you?"

"Not so much." He paused in front of the counter laden with old newspapers. "What's with the disaster zone?"

"Uncle Milton's a packrat. Saves everything."

Craig flopped down uninvited into the chair in front of her desk. "How do you work in this chaos?"

Sighing, Ali plopped the stack of mail on a pile of magazines and took off her coat. After tossing the garment over a heap of boxes, she dropped into her chair in front of her laptop. "Like this. A monitor, a full coffee cup, and I'm focused. Nothing else matters. No one else matters." She glared at him, hoping he'd take the hint and leave.

"Unless they write you letters, huh?" Craig smirked. "Or maybe love letters wouldn't have irritated you quite as much."

His masculine tones washed over her like effervescent water rushing over her skin. Ugh. She needed to emasculate the thought of him and her, of him as a romantic interest, from her mind. Nothing was going to happen between them. She was in Basalt Bay to do a job—a job people didn't like based upon those rude letters. When Uncle Milton returned, she'd be leaving. No time to start up a relationship.

Besides, Craig's vest labeled "Basalt Bay Jail" was a stark reminder of his bad character. Why would she want to be with a guy like him? He was obviously trouble.

Gorgeous trouble. Intriguing trouble.

His dark, somber moods probably rivaled her own. What a duo they'd make. Despite her internal arguments, thinking of them as a couple captivated her thoughts. Lulled her into imagining things she shouldn't be imagining. But soon, she'd be heading back to her posh desk in Portland. He'd be nothing but a memory, again.

"Is there anything else?" she asked coolly.

"You're ice and fire, aren't you?"

"Don't toy with me."

"Not toying. Stating facts. But don't worry, your tender side fascinates me enough to overcome any disparity your ice queen glares create." He smirked again.

She fought a smile. His eloquence rivaled a writer's words. Rivaled her own thoughts.

"About the letters?" He nodded to the pile. "Who sent them?"

"Do you think I would have asked you if I knew? Paige stopped by and—"

"Paige?" he yelped.

Her reporter's reflexes ignited. Why the interest in Forest's wife? Did Craig have feelings for her? A past relationship? Maybe something for her to research. Not that she wanted to cause him emotional pain. The detective? He was a cog in the corrupt mechanisms in Basalt Bay. That was what her uncle uncovered—or what his source uncovered. He was fair game.

"What does she have to do with anything?" Craig asked in a more normal tone.

"She wants to write a—" Privileged information. Or was it?

"What does she want to write?" Craig leaned forward, muscled forearms resting against the massive desk.

"An article vindicating her precious hubby." The words burned across her lips. She was usually better at keeping private information private. But she still resented Forest Harper.

Craig squinted at her. "You think she had something to do with the letters?"

"Possibly. I thought the detective might know something." She checked the time on her phone. She needed to get busy. She had to write a blistering editorial response to those letters. Nothing less would do.

"He obviously didn't. Same as me." Craig spread out his hands. "Were the letters unkind?"

"Look, I have work to do."

"Sure, you do." He hooked his thumbs in the armholes of his vest and slouched in the chair as if he planned to spend the day right there. "So do I." His wide grin said he wouldn't be bullied or affected by anything she said to him.

"Maybe you stirred up Paige to retaliate against me." She let her voice take on a snide tone. "Against my uncle's paper."

"I did no such thing. Why would I go to that much trouble for someone who obviously despises me?"

Despises him? Yeah, right.

At least his smirking and grinning at her vanished. Good. She had important things to do. Starting with getting this Don Juan out of her temporary office. If he stayed too long, she might imagine ways to be with him, going on a real date to find out where this ... whatever this was between them ... might lead.

Too bad long-distance relationships held no interest for her. She was a career woman. On the go. How could she ever settle down in a small hamlet like this?

"Do you want to go out with me?"

She nearly fell off her chair. "Why would I want to do that?"

"Glutton for punishment. New in town. Might need a friend."

"What, you and me becoming buddies?"

"Why not?" He grinned but there was a strain in his eyes.

Friends, huh? Enemies to lovers, maybe. But she wasn't settling down in this hole in the wall even for a winter dalliance with eye candy like Craig.

"Would going out with me be so bad?" His tone sounded vulnerable.

Denial was on the tip of her tongue, because if she dared to be honest with him, she'd surely regret it. Leaving a man she had a crush on for most of her life would be difficult enough. What would he say if she admitted to him that, yes, going on with her career choices once she knew the delicacies of his lips, of being held in his strong arms, would be terrible? No, she couldn't bear that. Better to have never loved.

"I'm sorry. I can't get involved."

"Involved," he spit out. Shoving away from the desk, he strode to the door. "Sorry for taking up your valuable time, Al."

"I—"

The door slammed.

If he was angry with her, good. Then he'd leave her alone. Why did that make her feel sad? Go on a date with him? Not a chance.

Yet, what if she'd simply said yes?

Seventeen

Inside the Basalt Bay City Clerk's office, Ruby read through old records, hoping to find a mailing address for the previous owners of the project house. Then she could send the photographs to them and be done with the task. So far, nothing.

After this, Peter was going to pick her up for a drive along the coast. Being alone with him sounded delightful. But her reason for requesting this outing made her nervous. Kissing him was fine and good. But without an honest-to-goodness, bare-your-heart talk, where was their relationship leading them?

She knew where—into the danger zone, into intimacy. She couldn't let that happen until they'd talked through their problems. Until they'd come to some real agreement as marriage partners.

"Are you finding what you need?" The clerk, "Sandy" according to her nametag, tapped her wristwatch. "We're about to close for lunch."

"You're closing?"

"Every day at noon."

Ruby groaned. "I didn't know. Sorry." She sent a text to Peter telling him to pick her up at twelve instead of twelve-thirty. That meant she'd get to be with him sooner. Their talk would commence sooner too.

Flipping through a couple more pages, she found the names Phil and Annie Peterson, owners of the property from 1938 until 1999. Their daughter, Jennifer Richards, had inherited the place. No forwarding address. Bess, Callie, and Kathleen were listed as the current owners.

"I'm sorry, but it's closing time." Sandy gave Ruby a rueful smile. "Come back at one o'clock if you'd like."

Ruby handed the ledger to her. "Thanks for letting me look through this."

"That's what we're here for."

Except from noon to one, right? Ah, well. At least Ruby found some names to look up on the internet. Was Jennifer Richards still alive? Would she be interested in the pictures from the attic?

A wide smile on his face, Peter pulled up in front of the office building in his rental car.

Ruby slid into the passenger seat. "Thanks for coming over sooner."

"Sure. I've been looking forward to this all morning." He grinned like a boy about to go on an adventure.

"Me too." Although the reason she wanted to come on this drive was probably far different from the one he was hoping for.

"You're quiet," he said after he drove a dozen miles down Highway 101. "Did you get bad news?"

"It isn't that."

"What's bothering you?"

Their gazes met. His attention drifted back to the road.

Would pushing for a discussion ruin their romantic outing if she was honest with him from the get-go?

Suddenly, he braked and swerved into a pull-out overlooking the waves crashing against the seashore below. He shut off the engine. "Ruby, we need to talk."

"Oh?" His bringing up their impending conversation surprised her. "Okay."

"After our walk the other day, and after our kisses, clearing the air has been on my mind."

"I'm glad to hear it." Maybe this drive would turn out better than she thought.

"Rube, I love you so much." Reaching across the console, he took her in his arms and kissed her passionately.

She went along with the kissing, enjoying his mouth's soft movements against hers, but her curiosity was piqued. What did Peter want to discuss? After a minute of smooching with him, she settled back into her seat, facing him, her hands clasped together, ready for their talk.

A serious expression crossed his face. "I miss what you and I were as a married couple before all the problems happened between us. I miss us."

"Me too," she said quietly.

"I am sorry for letting things fester between us." His throaty words sounded like they were expelled from the depths of him. "And for excluding you. I never meant for that to happen."

"Why did you let things, as you said, fester between us without talking about them?"

Leaning his forearms over the top of the steering wheel, he sighed. "My dad's the silent type, stubborn and brooding. I'm just like him."

"Peter." She wanted to chuckle. "You are not your dad. Yes, you favor him. But just because he doesn't like to face things doesn't mean you can't face things. You're a grown man who can live anyway you choose."

"Yeah, but it's what I grew up around. His noncommunicative ways are all I've known in a man."

Ruby didn't want to argue with him. "Since you've been living with him, have you two talked?"

"Just about sports, the weather, fixing up the old house. I'd like to help him before I—"

She guessed what he'd almost said. Before he returned to the *Lily Forever*. Was that what prompted this discussion? Was he opening up to her with the intention of asking her to go north with him sooner? Kiss her like crazy until she was weak all the way through her body, then try to fix things in a rush and coax her back to his boat?

No, that wasn't going to work. A fire slow-burned inside of her. If Peter was acting emotional just to hoodwink her into going back to Alaska with him, she didn't appreciate his efforts at all!

"When we planned on coming for this drive, I wanted us to talk," she said tightly.

"I figured." He stared out toward the ocean, not meeting her gaze. "Dad says I'm the man. It's up to me to work things out. To go along with—"

"Go along with what?" She hardly recognized the sharp tone of voice that came out of her.

"That I should go along with whatever you want to make peace."

"What? You can't be serious!"

"What's wrong with that?" He glanced at her. "It got us talking, didn't it?"

"Yeah. But are you talking to me because your father said to, and not because you feel like talking is the right thing to do?" A dark shadow crossed his gaze, and she knew the answer. "You don't mean to truly work things out with me, do you? Is this a game to you, Peter?"

"What? No!"

"Are you promising me things you don't plan to follow through on? Kissing me and trying to convince me of your love, then go on living like you always have?"

"Ruby—"

"Turn around. I want to go back to the project house."

"Why? Why are you so mad at me?"

"This was a mistake. We're not ready for this talk." She thrust out her hands. "And we're done kissing! I mean it."

"I do want to talk with you."

"If you're going along with what I want just to make things easier on you, not really to fix anything, you're not ready for this conversation. Nor for this relationship! We're done."

"I want us to talk. It's not just because—"

"Fine." She yanked on the door handle. "I'll walk back."

He groaned and started the engine.

She shut the door.

All the way back to the project house, she stared out the passenger side window, not making eye contact with Peter, keeping her arms crossed over her ribs. She should never have given into kissing him until they'd had a real talk.

Eighteen

Peter gripped the steering wheel so tightly, if it were made of wood, he'd have broken it in two. He couldn't believe how his conversation with Ruby turned out. She thought he was milking her with sweet talk just to get her to do what he wanted? He'd been honest, hadn't he? Sure, he may have poured on the syrup a little thick and did what his dad suggested. Why did she take such offense? How was he ever going to figure her out? How could he get beyond her defenses?

He pulled to a stop in front of the project house. Ruby opened the door immediately. He hopped out, rushing ahead of her on the trail.

"Please, wait." He held out his hands to her, but she trounced around him, not slowing down. "Ruby!"

At the stairs, she paused and looked downward, not meeting his gaze. "Until you can come up with a better reason for making things right between us than going along with something lame your father told you to do, stay away from me. We both need more time to think."

"Time." He groaned. "You're the one who wanted to talk! Now you're angry at me for talking?"

She lifted her eyes, and her face was a mottled color. She looked in pain.

"Are you all right?"

"No, I'm not all right! I've waited for things to get better between us. After our kisses on the beach, even in the car, I hoped—" She groaned. "It doesn't matter."

"I'm sorry, okay?" He reached for her, but she jerked away from him. "What? I don't even know what to do to make you happy anymore."

"Make me happy?" The words exploded out of her. "Have I asked you to make me happy?"

"Uh. Yeah. Sort of." He rubbed his hand over the base of his neck.

"Then you don't understand the first thing about me." A vein beneath her eye twitched. "All this time I thought you were here to try to understand me, and us, better."

"Of course that's why I'm here." He pulsed his hands toward the project house. "Why else would I work like a dog with you? Doing whatever you wanted? Trying to please you?"

"Please me? Please me?" she repeated loudly as if he might not have heard her the first time.

"I guess I failed at that too, like everything else." He pinched the bridge of his nose.

"Don't you dare give me that wounded puppy garbage!" She thrust out her index finger toward him. "You chose to marry me, but then you didn't like the responsibility of trying to stay married to me."

"Not true!" Every problem in their marriage wasn't his fault. "I want to be married to you. I'll do whatever it takes for us to stay married. That's why I came back, isn't it?"

"Then prove it."

"Whaaaaaat?"

"If you want to stay married to me, prove it."

"Prove it how?"

"What are you willing to do for us to continue in this relationship?"

"Didn't I already prove that?" he thundered. "I came to Basalt, twice, to be with you!"

"This is about the rest of our lives together, Peter. Or not." Tears welled in her eyes. "Prove that you want to be married to me, if you do."

"I—" How could he do what she asked when he didn't even know how he'd stuck his foot in his mouth so badly already? "I will." Gritty determination filled him. "I will prove myself to you."

"Not just yourself."

"What do you want from me?" he bellowed.

"You. I want you, Peter Cedars. Not"—she gulped like she was fighting those tears—"half of you. Not the you who says what I want you to say to make things right. You! Your whole heart, being, body, self."

"Ruby—"

"Until you figure that out, until you find enough love in you, and you know what you're willing to do to put your full weight into our marriage, stay away from me."

He couldn't believe this.

She turned on her heel and strode inside the project house, slamming the door. The lock clunked loudly.

His groan turned into a thundering howl, reaching the trees, the skies. But releasing his anger made him feel better. Now, how in the world was he going to prove his love to his wife?

Nineteen

Forest synced the app on his phone to be able to listen in on the conversation Deputy Brian was about to have with Mia. He'd watched the last video of her visiting Evie's cell but hadn't witnessed an exchange of mail. Twice, Evie turned away from the camera. Maybe she tucked a letter in the book then.

Could he have been wrong about all this? If today's sting went bust, he might have to accept that Mia wasn't the guilty party he suspected her of being. A harsh pill to swallow. But he couldn't keep beating the same drum, especially when he was no longer employed by the task force.

"All set?" Brian asked as he entered the office from the restroom.

"Yes."

Brian tapped something on his phone. "You should get out of here."

"Right."

They'd discussed this. If Forest was present, Mia might not do whatever she normally did to transfer communications.

That's probably what happened the day he barged into the deputy's office demanding to check the library books. Had she hidden a note in her back pocket? Or tucked it in her purse?

Forest stepped into the interrogation room and dropped onto the floor in front of the door where it would be difficult for her to see him. He put the earbud in his ear.

He heard the creak of the outer door opening.

"Hey, Deputy!" Mia said in her wispy voice.

"How's it going, Mia?" Did Brian's voice warble? Was he nervous about this covert operation?

"I'm doing good." Mia gave a teasing laugh. "Why, Deputy, you are such a strong, handsome man. Just feel those muscles!"

Was she touching the deputy's biceps? A lip smacking sound followed. What was going on out there?

Forest moved slightly, bumping the door. He held his breath.

"Did you hear something?" Mia asked.

"Not me," Deputy Brian said. "Are you dropping off books today?"

"I sure am. Evie loves her romances. Swallows them up like a canary gobbling seeds. I like romance too." There was her flirty tone again. "It's been a long time since you and I"— she giggled—"spent time together."

Her and Deputy Brian? Forest scowled.

"Now, now. You and I never—"

"Look at you blush. Don't worry. It was only one date. I don't kiss and tell." Her heels click-clacked across the floor.

A door opened, shut.

Forest blew out the breath he'd been holding.

"Ignore the last part," Brian muttered into the listening device.

Right. If Brian and Mia dated, their relationship wasn't any of his business. Might have been years ago. Still, that explained why Brian seemed like putty in Mia's hands. Why he nominated her as interim mayor. Did he harbor a crush for the flirty receptionist?

The next ten minutes felt like the longest in his life as Forest waited for Mia to reenter the office.

"Hey, Deputy," her voice finally came through the speaker. "Evie and I got to talking. Where did the time go?"

"Are those the books you're returning to the library?" Deputy Brian asked.

Hopefully, he would follow the plan he and Forest discussed.

"Sure are. Like I said, Evie is a voracious reader."

"Strange thing is I haven't seen her reading."

Good. Deputy Brian was proceeding as planned.

"What's that?" Mia's voice rose.

"She watches TV. Scritch-scratches in a journal. No reading."

"I'm sure you're mistaken." Mia laughed nervously. Her heels clunked across the floor.

Forest wanted to jump up and stop her from exiting, but he waited for the deputy to make the next move.

"I'm sorry, Mia. But I have to ask to check those library books."

"Check them for what?"

"It's my new policy," Brian said without his voice waffling. "All library books must be checked by me from now on."

"I don't understand," Mia said in a whiny voice. "Next you'll be wanting to search me too." She huffed. "Deputy Brian!"

"Stop right there!"

"Leave me alone!"

Forest stood and peered out the corner of the window. Brian and Mia both held opposite ends of a book and were tugging on it. Mia grimaced. Brian looked equally determined.

"Let me have the book!"

"No! It's not your business."

Forest scrambled into the office. "Need any help, Deputy?"

"What are you doing here?" Mia screeched.

"Nope." Brian yanked the book free just as an envelope dropped out. Mia lunged to the floor, her hands flailing for the loose envelope like it was a hundred-dollar bill she didn't want to lose.

Forest wanted to dive on the floor and retrieve it himself.

Brian dropped to his knees and yanked the envelope from Mia's fingers. Holding it high, he stood while she reached for the paper.

"Give that back! It's private property!"

"Everything coming or going from this office is mine to inspect."

Good job, Deputy!

"I can't believe you'd turn on me like this!" Mia stamped her foot.

"It's nothing personal." Brian was already opening the letter. "It's addressed to Edward."

"Of course, it is!" Mia strummed her hands frantically through her hair. "He's going to be enraged that you dared to read his mail."

"Is this how you communicated with Edward while he was in jail here?" Forest demanded. "Hiding notes in books? In your clothes, perhaps?"

Her face hued red. "I'm not discussing anything about what I did, or didn't do, with you." She glared hotly at Brian. "If you know what's good for you, you'll hand me the letter now!"

"Are you threatening the deputy?" Forest asked.

"If he doesn't listen, he'll be sorry." She trounced to the door, her long hair lifting and falling with each step. "Don't forget. Your job is on the line." She stomped outside and slammed the door.

Forest wanted to clap handcuffs on her wrists and detain her, but he couldn't. He stared at the closed door. "Isn't there something we can book her for?"

"On what charge?" Brian waved the confiscated paper in the air. "It's a love letter."

"What about her passing threats to people in town?"

"Nothing actionable." Brian sat down at the desk, peering at the letter. "I'll submit my report to Sheriff Morris. See what he says."

Forest followed him to the desk. "What did she mean about your job being on the line? Has she threatened you before?"

"Just drop it." Brian sucked in a breath. "Check out the small print at the bottom of the page. Isn't this identical to the print on the letter attached to the rock you submitted last month?"

Forest clasped the page that appeared ripped from a journal and squinted at the lettering. In tiny one-sixteenth-inch print, the lightly written words, "It will happen at the art gala," leaped out at him.

The threat felt like a kick in his gut.

Someone was still planning something bad for Paige's gallery opening? What had Evie told Paige about the event? *"Accidents can happen so quickly."* Adrenaline shot up Forest's spine, churning ice cold in his veins.

"Do you think Mia knows about this?" Brian asked, his tone subdued.

"Yeah, I do. I think she's had her finger in everything that's gone down so far." But how was he going to prove that before Edward's trial?

Twenty

With the *Gazette* clutched tightly in one hand, Paige rapped on her aunt's first-floor bedroom door with the other hand. "Aunt Callie, can I speak with you?"

"Just a minute."

"Okay. Hurry, please."

In a few minutes she had to open the gallery, but this couldn't wait. She strode past the wooden stairway, pausing to admire the repairs Forest had done with the handrailing. His craftsmanship was like a work of art!

The bedroom door opened, and Aunt Callie shuffled out in slippers and a robe. "What's this about, Paige?"

"Sorry to bother you so early. Yesterday, Alison Riley confronted Forest at Bert's."

"Did she now?" Aunt Callie chuckled. "She wasn't too happy?"

"You could say that." Paige held up the newspaper. "It seems my idea backfired. And I haven't told Forest about the letter-writing scheme being my idea."

"Let's go in here, and you can tell me all about it." Aunt

Callie linked her arm with Paige's and drew her toward the dining room table.

After both were seated, Paige opened the paper to the editorial section. "See what she wrote."

Aunt Callie clasped the newspaper and squinted toward the page, clearly in need of her reading glasses. "'An outcry of letters to the editor demands a response,'" she read A. Riley's article out loud. "'My official answer is no! I will not write a retraction. I'm a writer. Not a pal who accepts advice, or coercion, about my subject matter. This is how the news works, people! Get used to it. For the record, unsigned letters to the editor will not be published!'" Aunt Callie groaned. "She is one hard nut to crack."

"Did we go too far with the shower of letters?"

"Not even close. We've only begun to battle journalistic tyranny!"

Paige held up her hands in protest. "I'm afraid Forest will be unhappy to hear of my involvement with this."

"Did you write any of the letters?" Aunt Callie tapped her finger against the tabletop.

"No."

"Then there's nothing for him to be unhappy about, is there?"

"I don't know." Paige had gotten cold feet about writing a letter to the editor herself. Besides being busy with the gallery opening, she dreaded the thought of going against anything Forest didn't want her to do. Yet doing nothing settled in her throat like a bad case of strep. She'd skirted her own participation by passing off the letter-writing campaign to Aunt Callie. Look how that turned out!

"You should write something." Aunt Callie smoothed her finger over the paper's edge. "This woman has declared war on the people of our town willing to stand up for one of our own."

"Do you mean it? Are you claiming Forest as one of our own?"

"He's your husband, isn't he? Your real husband, now?" Aunt Callie gazed intently at her.

"Yes, he is. I love him."

Aunt Callie patted her cheek. "Then, yes, I'll claim him as one of our own. If he makes you happy, I'm happy. Even though Alison says she won't budge, it sounds like she read the letters."

"Read them, but was unmoved by them?"

"Exactly." Aunt Callie's eyes brightened. "I think it's your turn. You should write a letter that comes straight from your heart!"

Paige pressed her lower lip between her teeth. "I'm having second thoughts." Squeamish, intimidating, worrisome second thoughts.

"If it was me—"

"You'd go right in there and tell Alison exactly how you feel. I tried that, in my own way." She glanced away from Aunt Callie's gaze. "It didn't work out so well. I must decide the rest for myself. Thank you for helping with the letter-writing campaign, though."

"Maybe Bess could speak with Alison? Surely, the bull-headed journalist would have to listen to our mayor."

"We shouldn't involve Bess. It's a conflict of interest." Paige folded the newspaper. "She's my business partner and Paisley's mother-in-law."

"Fine. The letters were only phase one." Aunt Callie held up her index finger. "We need to move the dial in our favor with Milton's niece, or else move her out of Basalt Bay!"

"That doesn't sound very Christ-like of us." In fact, this whole lettering-writing business was weighing heavily on Paige's conscience.

"Sometimes you must take matters into your own hands." Aunt Callie gave her a knowing grin. "Write your letter. Something you say might make a difference."

Paige sighed. "Maybe we should let it rest until after Christmas. Until after the trial." By then Forest might be able to comment too.

"I'll think of something." Aunt Callie puckered her lips like she was chewing on an idea.

"I have to go open the gallery." Paige stood and kissed her aunt's cheek.

"May I keep the paper?"

"Sure. What are you going to do?"

"Maybe it's best if you don't know."

The expression on Aunt Callie's face said she had a scheme up her sleeve that Paige probably wasn't going to like. What had she started?

Twenty-one

The front door creaked open, breaking Ali's zombie-like stare toward the computer screen. An older woman with some plumpness to her girth strode into the office, a scowl lining her face.

"Are you A. Riley?"

One of those letter writers, no doubt.

"I am. And you are?"

"Callie Cedars." The woman tugged her purse over her shoulder in jerky motions. "Got a minute?"

"Well, I—"

"Sure, you do." Callie settled heavily into the chair opposite Ali.

Cedars, huh? Paige's aunt?

"What can I help you with, ma'am?" Was she here to demand a retraction too?

"Where's Milton?" Callie lifted her chin. "I'd rather speak with the man in charge."

"He's away."

"As in ran away?" Callie snorted. "If something smells fishy, it usually is."

"I assure you there's nothing—" Ali cleared her throat. She wasn't going to lie to this woman. Her uncle's business was his own. However, Callie's glare had an unnerving quality that made Ali want to squirm. "How do you know my uncle?"

"I've lived in Basalt Bay my whole life. There are few residents I don't know."

"Are you friends with the Grants?" Maybe Ali could veer this conversation in a direction that would benefit her.

"If you mean Edward, no." Callie adjusted herself in the wooden chair. "Bess is my friend. Judah's my niece's husband."

"How long did you know Edward before he became mayor?" Ali picked up her pen to jot a few notes.

Callie pegged her with a dark stare.

Ali dropped the pen. "Is there something you need, Ms. Cedars?"

"What will it take for you to write a withdrawal of your statements concerning my niece's husband?"

So, that's why she was here. What was with these people?

"I won't be writing one of those any time soon."

"Why not?" Callie bared her teeth slightly. "It's Christmastime in a town that's suffered this year. Why add to the turmoil with mistruths in our paper?"

"Mistruths?" The word burned in her throat. "My uncle—"

"Milton seems like an honest man who wouldn't allow this rubbish to be expunged in his newspaper!"

Expunged, indeed.

"My uncle left me with full editorial control. Anything I say about the town—"

"What did he tell you about our town? About Edward?"

Ali gnawed on the inside of her cheek. Didn't Uncle Milton say Basalt Bay was full of gossips and backstabbers? Maybe he'd include the woman sitting across from her in his assessment.

"Don't want to talk about it? Easier to cast darts with words?" Callie settled her arms over the edge of the desk. "How about a trade, then?"

"What kind of trade?" A barter? Blackmail?

"You write an article explaining your false opinions about Forest Harper and I'll give you something you want."

"Such as?" Ali sat up straighter, her reporter's brain firing on all cylinders.

"A Basalt Bay history lesson?"

"Including information about Edward?" Eagerness flitted through her. "You're saying if I write a retraction"—which she wasn't agreeing to—"you'll answer *all* my questions?"

"Not all. I'm not that much of a blabbermouth!"

"No?"

Callie's posture stiffened.

"Sorry." Ali didn't want to offend the woman who might have the information she needed to write a breaking news story about Edward, maybe even about Bess. "When can we start?" She rubbed her hands together.

"When will you pen an apology?"

"Apology? A retraction isn't an apology."

"In my book, it is." Callie pushed out of the chair. "Let me know when you change your mind."

"Wait. Can't we discuss this some more?"

Ali couldn't let a gold mine like Callie Cedars slip through her fingers. Her quest to find out the truth about Uncle Milton's involvement with the deposed mayor might depend on this woman's knowledge.

But writing an apology? That was asking too much.

Twenty-two

Judah hauled a pile of two-by-eight hemlock boards from his truck down to the spot on the beach where the gazebo used to sit before the structure was smashed to smithereens. Forest would be here any minute to help him carry materials and to build a similar shelter. Spring would have been a better time for this project. Warmer, at least. But Paisley had been persuasive. With her nearly begging him to build the gazebo before Christmas, how could he refuse?

Her idea of Forest and Paige having their ceremony here sounded cool. And while he'd asked Forest to assist with the build, Judah told him to keep the plans to himself. He wanted to introduce the idea of the Christmas Eve vow renewal to him in person.

He dropped his pile of boards onto the sand. Then went back to the truck for another load.

On his second time dropping off materials, a car engine shut off. A few minutes later, Forest strode toward him with a piece of paper extended in his hand. "I got the permit to rebuild the gazebo you requested."

"That's great!" Judah had ins with the mayor's office, but he wanted to go through the proper channels. "Any problems?"

"None whatsoever. The clerk seemed enthusiastic about us bringing the landmark back to life." Forest chuckled. "It was as if the gazebo were an old friend."

"I can see why. I proposed to Paisley here."

"So I heard." Forest clapped him on the back. "That's why I asked Paige to marry me again here where the gazebo used to be, also."

They went back to Judah's truck and grabbed the rest of the lumber and tools.

"Hey, what was with the 'don't tell Paige about this' business?" Forest asked as they dropped off the load with the other boards.

"Paisley has an idea I want to run by you." Judah dug a few tools out of his toolbox. "Are you still planning to recite your vows again?"

"Uh-huh. Paige is up to her ears in work, so she wants to wait until January." Forest frowned. "With the trial coming up, maybe even February. Why? What's Paisley's idea?"

Judah swept some sand off the old cement cornerstone. "No pressure. But she thought it would be fun to spring a surprise on Paige with a Christmas Eve vow renewal right here."

"You're kidding."

"Nope. I guess she's feeling sentimental. Wanted to do something nice for Paige. You, too, of course."

"Actually, that's brilliant." Forest tugged a pair of gloves out of his pockets and put them on. "A Christmas surprise? I like it!"

"You're sure?"

"Absolutely. A Christmas Eve wedding under the stars?" Forest spread his arms toward the sky. "Surprising my wife with a gift she'll never forget? What could be better?"

"We could have a toasty bonfire."

"Sounds great. My parents will be here. My sister, too. Perfect timing."

"So, you're in?"

"Yeah, I am." Forest sighed. "With some case stuff troubling me, I could use a distraction."

"Anything you want to discuss?"

"Not until I know more." Forest pointed toward the lumber stack. "What do we do first?"

"Let's line up these boards with the cement corners. We'll attach these brackets. Easy as pie." Judah held up the metal pieces he'd purchased.

"Will do."

Two hours later, they'd built the twelve-by-twelve-foot floor with corner beams in place. Even the arched rafters went up without much difficulty. A few more hours of work, a coat of stain, and this gazebo would be ready for a vow renewal ceremony and a new season of announcements and celebrations for their family and the community, too.

Twenty-three

Peter and Dad had their routines which usually kept them out of each other's hair. Peter got up early and drank several cups of coffee before showering. A half-hour later, Dad typically shuffled downstairs and sat at the kitchen table, drinking his coffee and reading the paper. If their paths crossed, they remained quiet, not saying "good morning," or asking about each other's day, which was perfectly fine with Peter.

Since his disastrous drive and talk with Ruby two days ago, he kept to himself more, even bringing his coffee up to his room so Dad wouldn't pester him with questions. "Where's Ruby?" "Why haven't I seen your lovely wife lately?" "When are you two getting back together?" Peter could do without such comments.

Ruby wanted proof of his love. What herculean effort would he have to do to satisfy her demands? Give her his kidney? Sell the *Lily Forever*? He groaned loudly. Who did Ruby think she was to require such a thing of him? The tempest in his brain made his heart race, and his temples felt like they might explode.

She didn't say get rid of the boat.

That's right. He expelled a breath. She didn't say that.

He fixed himself another cup of coffee. Maybe he could slip upstairs without Dad talking to him. He hustled over to the stairway.

"What are you up to today?" Dad asked.

Peter clenched his jaw and paused, one foot on the first step. "Not much."

Since Ruby didn't want to see him, he had too much time on his hands, which made him miss his boat even more.

"When are the two of you going to start acting like a married couple?" Dad adjusted the black glasses on his nose.

"Good question." Not planning to discuss his marriage with his father, he asked lightly, "Trying to get rid of me already?"

"Not even. But I like Ruby."

"Yeah." Peter heaved a sigh. "I do too."

"Then what are you going to do about it?" Dad's voice rose. "You're the man. It's up to you to take the lead in these matters."

Not that again! Weren't those the exact opinions that got him into trouble with Ruby? "Since when are you an expert on marriage?"

"I've watched a fair share of Oprah and Dr. Phil." Chuckling, Dad set down his paper.

"Our problems will take more than TV expertise to fix."

"I'm sure. Care for some advice?" Dad pushed his black glasses farther up his nose.

No thanks! But he didn't object out loud. Why was his father pushing him? Did Ruby talk to him? Did they sit down and plot together how to get him to do things her way? Fresh irritation pummeled through him.

"When your mother and I argued, sometimes we wouldn't talk for weeks. I slept on the couch plenty of times." His face turned ruddy as if he was embarrassed admitting it. "You and I don't talk about these things, but it's been on my mind."

Peter shuffled his weight back and forth. Let his father get whatever he needed to say off his chest, then he'd head upstairs or take a beach walk, anything to get away from talking about this.

"Want to know what made peace between us, finally?" Dad's eyebrows rose. Apparently, he was waiting for Peter's response.

"No." He sighed. "What?"

"Me getting off my high horse."

Peter clenched his jaw. Was Dad calling him prideful? Was he saying the troubles between him and Ruby were all his fault?

"Your mom would get mad. I reverted into my shell—so deep no one could find me, especially her."

"I, uh, need to go do something." Peter strode across the kitchen, set his cup in the sink, then grabbed his coat off a hook. "Talk to you later."

"I see myself in you."

Peter's stride came to a halt.

"The fight. The bluster to be right. Keeping the weight of the world buried within. I was like that too." Dad drew in a shaky breath. "I could fight with your mom all day. Kind of like how I do with Callie. Or I could make peace."

So, he was weak like Peter thought.

"I refused to leave her." Dad's voice took on a determined tone. "I stayed and made things right the best I could."

Peter wanted to stomp out the door. But part of him wanted to stay and hear what his father had to say, whether he liked the advice or not.

"Were you happy?" Ruby acted weirdly upset when he told her he was trying to make her happy.

"What does being happy have to do with anything?" Dad asked.

Sure sounded like he and Ruby shared notes.

"Everything? Who doesn't want happiness in their marriage? In their love life?"

"Peace." Dad patted his chest. "That's what mattered to me."

"So, you caved for the sake of peace?" Peter scoffed. "Didn't you get to decide how you lived your own life?"

Dad made a grumbling sound and folded the newspaper as if the conversation were finished.

Peter was just getting good and riled. Some of his anger with Ruby may have come out toward his father. "Why didn't you stand up for what you wanted?"

"You expect happiness without effort?" Dad eyed him sternly like he did when Peter was a boy and hadn't done an expected chore. "Without putting yourself fully in the game?"

"I don't think you're one to talk to me about a successful marriage. You and Mom acted like you hated each other most of the time."

Dad winced.

"Mom yelled at you, and you did everything she said?" The words tumbled out of him, his voice escalating in volume.

"Let her punish me and Paisley in inappropriate ways, and you did nothing? All for your precious peace?"

Tears flooded his father's eyes. He stared hard at the table, not meeting Peter's gaze.

"Uh—" Should he apologize? Say he didn't mean it? "That was harsh. I'm sorry."

"It's probably been eating at you for a long time," Dad said quietly. "Paisley mentioned this to me also. So, you think I'm to blame for your failed marriage?"

"Of course not. I'm to blame for my own shortcomings." Although, he cursed his father and mother more times than he wanted to admit for some of his failings. "I'm just saying—" Why say anything? Why make things worse between him and his dad?

"What?" Dad pushed away from the table and stood. "Go ahead. Get it off your chest. Then maybe you and Ruby can move forward."

"Did she talk with you?"

"When?"

"Yesterday. Today. Did you and Ruby talk over how to get me to do things her way?" His accusing tone blasted out.

"I haven't spoken to her in a week." Dad heaved a sigh. "If I did, I'd tell her the same thing. Keep working on your relationship. Nothing will get better unless you do."

"I've got to go. " Peter had heard enough. He strode out of the house, letting the door slam behind him.

All the way down to City Beach, then the mile of trudging north along the seashore, his thoughts churned with what Dad said, mixed with what Ruby said to him two days ago. "Prove it," repeated over and over in his thoughts in his wife's voice.

He wasn't ready to try talking to her yet. But maybe, if he had a conversation with someone who understood marriage and reconciliation, he might get some clarity. Perhaps, some sympathy.

Talking with his father had only frustrated him more.

Twenty-four

Paisley followed Judah down the sandy beach at Baker's Point, staring at the sand without peeking at anything else like he'd instructed her to do. Even though she already guessed what he was about to show her, excitement pulsated through her veins. He and Forest must have finished the gazebo!

"You're not sneaking a look, are you?"

"No, I'm not." She laughed.

"Okay." His arm smoothed over her shoulder. "Here it is, sweetheart!"

She glanced up. "Oh, Judah."

The rustic wooden gazebo with its simple design looked so much like the one she remembered from her childhood and young adulthood.

"It's beautiful. Thank you for doing this!" She kissed him, then threw her arms around his shoulders and hugged him. "You're the best. Seeing this structure gives me all the warm emotions of the day you asked me to marry you here when I was eighteen."

"Ah, Pais." He leaned her back and kissed her some more. She loved the feel of his arms around her. She rested her cheek against his chest.

"Everyone in town will be thrilled about this, too. It's a Christmas present for all of us. You've really done a nice thing."

"I can't take all the credit. Forest helped too."

Judah clasped her hand and led her toward the gazebo where she and others would make future announcements for their families.

Please, God, let there be a baby for me to tell Judah about.

She'd been so tempted to tell him a dozen times already. Each time, she cautioned herself to wait until she was certain. After several previous miscarriages, she was nervous about even taking the test and possibly facing a negative result. But come Christmas Eve morning, she'd take the test and tell him that night.

As soon as they reached the corner post that smelled of freshly stained wood, Paisley froze at the sight of a woman curled up in a sleeping bag on the gazebo floor. The stranger stared back at them with sad, tired-looking eyes.

Judah gripped Paisley's hand. "Who are you? Why are you here?"

The dark-haired woman wiped strands of shoulder-length hair off her face. "It was inviting. The sea. The shelter." Sitting up, she yawned and ran her gloved hands over her coat-clad arms.

"It must have been cold last night." Relaxing a little, Paisley released her hand from Judah's. The woman had to be in dire circumstances to be sleeping on the beach in December. "Do you need help? Are you okay?"

"You won't turn me in, will you? I'll get up and leave right now. I promise I won't bother you."

"Turn you into whom?" Paisley asked.

"The law. Who else?"

"Are you running from the law?" Judah frowned.

"No. But I've been chased from beaches before." The woman coughed. "Towns don't usually like homeless people sleeping on their property."

Paisley met Judah's gaze and silently appealed to him. Wasn't there something they could do? It was Christmastime. This woman obviously needed assistance.

"What's your name?" Paisley asked.

"Sarah."

"Hi, Sarah. I'm Paisley. This is my husband, Judah."

"Hello," she said in a raspy, dry-sounding voice.

She looked to be in her late thirties. A bit ruffled by the conditions and her circumstances, perhaps, but her eyes were clear. She didn't appear to be on drugs, dangerous, or on the run from the law. Although, how could anyone be certain? What brought Sarah to this situation in life to be sleeping on the beach?

Paisley imagined her own race across the country when she left Basalt and fled to Chicago. She'd been desperate then. Was this woman running from something, or someone?

"Is there anything we can do for you? Anyone we can contact?"

"No." Sarah ran her hand over the zipper of her sleeping bag.

"Would you like some breakfast?" Judah asked. "There's a diner in town—Bert's Fish Shack. Great breakfast joint."

Paisley could have kissed him. "That's right. Will you let us buy you breakfast? Hot coffee sounds nice, huh?"

"Um, sure. But why would you buy my breakfast?" Sarah pulled deeper into the security of the sleeping bag, gazing at them warily. "You don't even know me."

"No, we don't. But I'm worried about you," Paisley said quietly. "We want to help you if we can."

"No one can help me." A grimace tugged the woman's lips downward. She scooted out of the sleeping bag in jerky movements, exposing her legs covered in thick dark leggings. She quickly rolled up her sleeping bag and attached it to the bottom of the pack as if she'd done it many times before. "Even so, I won't refuse a hot breakfast."

"That's good." Paisley nodded toward the stained wood above them. "My husband and my brother-in-law just built this gazebo."

"Uh-huh." Sarah glanced at Judah. "I saw them working here yesterday."

"You did?" he asked.

"I watched from behind those rocks over there." She lifted her chin toward a couple of large boulders. "I thanked God for providing a safe place for me to sleep."

"Oh, Sarah." Paisley's heart melted with compassion. "It's too cold to be sleeping outdoors. I'd like to help you find somewhere warmer to stay."

"I don't have money for a motel, or I would have stayed at the inn up the road."

"I have somewhere else in mind."

Paisley knew where Sarah might find a hot bath and a bed to sleep on tonight. She'd call Aunt Callie or Bess. Knowing how they wanted to help women who were down on their luck, she felt confident they'd invite Sarah to stay in the project house.

The idea of this woman sleeping on the beach, not having a home to go to, tugged at Paisley's heartstrings. She knew what being on the run felt like. Maybe that's why God brought Sarah to this spot where Paisley would find her.

Twenty-five

Craig sat in the noisy diner finishing his breakfast, not making eye contact with anyone. Since he frequented Bert's for meals, he'd gotten better at avoiding opinionated women like Maggie, Miss Patty, or Callie Cedars. He needed their advice like he needed a wardrobe of fluorescent green. He stuffed a bite of pancake in his mouth.

"Craig."

"Judah," he coughed out after he swallowed.

"Mind if I—" Judah dropped into the chair on the other side of the table without waiting for his approval.

Craig hoped to finish his breakfast and leave without speaking to anyone. That plan was foiled.

"We haven't spoken since we heard the news about our brotherhood." Judah drummed the edge of the table with his fingers. "Sorry you couldn't make it for Thanksgiving dinner. Paisley and I were disappointed."

Sure they were. Craig glanced away and saw Paisley sitting at a window seat across from a woman wearing a dirty, torn coat. Was she the same person Craig observed wearing an oversized backpack in town yesterday? He had a soft place in his heart for homeless folks, especially since he and his mom did their share of sleeping in their car when he was a kid.

He met Judah's gaze. Did he expect a response about the missed dinner? Surely, he hadn't meant for Craig to attend, considering their mutual past. He wasn't going to show up at a family gathering to placate anyone's sense of duty or familial responsibility, either.

"What will it take for us to work through the awkwardness?" Judah flexed his hand between them. "You and I can't help who our father is."

"Father," Craig spat out.

"He's that, even if neither of us cares to claim him right now." Judah shuffled a menu on the table back and forth. "Doesn't mean you and I can't be friends, brothers, even with everything that's transpired."

It was just like Judah to try to make some grand gesture. But did he mean what he said about being friends, brothers, considering all that happened between them? At least he wasn't trying to pretend none of the stuff in their past took place.

The clattering of plates and voices rose in the room. Had the surrounding noises become louder? Or were Craig's taut nerves making every jangle of silverware and clinking of glasses caused by the busser exaggerated?

"Can we?" One of Judah's eyebrows quirked. "Work out the other stuff?"

"I don't know. So much water under the bridge."

Couldn't he finish his breakfast in peace? He had to live in this town while he did his community service and attended anger management classes, nothing could be done about that. But he didn't have to cozy up to any of the residents— including this pseudo relative. But what if Judah really was extending friendship and brotherhood?

"Why even try?" Craig bit into a slice of bacon. Even if his stomach roiled over the current conversation, he wasn't going to let good food go to waste. That was something he learned as a poor kid with a single mom.

"Plenty of reasons." Judah linked his fingers together and heaved a sigh like he was settling in. "I believe in second chances. Especially between brothers."

Seriously? After all Craig did to sabotage Judah and Paisley's relationship? His job? He glanced across the diner to where Paisley chatted with the woman. Judah said he wanted them to have a familial tie, but what about his wife?

She was still beautiful. In the past, Craig was so attracted to her. Hadn't gotten over her for the longest time. But she was married to Judah, his previous friend, coworker, and eventual enemy. Now his brother? Time to put those old feelings behind him. Gritting his teeth, he hardened his determination to remain detached from the Grant and Cedars families.

"Look"—he pointed to his bright vest—"I'm here fulfilling my obligation to the state. Nothing more."

"You don't want us to be family, or to try to repair the damage? Is that what you're saying?"

"Isn't it obvious?" Craig glared at the man on the opposite side of the table. He didn't see any malice or anger on Judah's features, but he knew deep inside he had to be churning with angst over the things Craig had done—their fight on the beach, the problems at work, his making out with Paisley. Things that made Craig sick now. How could the past ever disappear? It would always be there to taunt and haunt him.

Best thing for him to do was to finish his assigned tasks and hightail it out of town. He was worthless to Judah and Paisley, Paige and Piper, too. They didn't need his brand of trouble.

Curiously, his gaze zinged back to Paisley and the woman. "What's with the vagrant?"

Judah glanced in the same direction. "I'm giving Paisley a few minutes to talk with her."

"Judah, the humanitarian, huh?" Craig said in a smirky tone. His fallback. Act tough, be tough—his method for getting through life.

"Something wrong with showing kindness now, too?" Judah's brows scrunched up.

"Just you being you, I guess." Craig fingered the condensation on his water glass.

"Listen, we'd like you to come over for Christmas Eve dinner. Consider this your official invitation to join our family for a holiday meal."

"We?" Craig's voice came out higher than usual. Not the tough-guy tone he tried to portray. "You're saying Paisley wants me to come over, too?" He guzzled from his water glass. His hand shook. Hopefully, Judah didn't notice. Being off the liquor still affected him.

"She does. Not with you sitting right next to her at the dinner table, mind you." His humor took some of the bite out of his words. "But you being there, all of us adjusting to our new family dynamics, accepting one another, would be meaningful to us." Judah shrugged. "What do you say? Would it kill you to show up and be friendly to the family? You can bring a plus-one."

Would showing up and being friendly to the family kill him? Maybe. A plus-one? If he went to a family dinner, which he doubted he'd do, he knew who he'd invite. But Al probably wouldn't be caught dead at a Grant/Cedars shindig.

It might be interesting, though.

Twenty-six

Paisley called ahead to speak with Aunt Callie about Sarah, but she wasn't home. When Kathleen answered the phone and heard about Sarah's predicament, her being the warm, loving person she was, she said, "Bring the dear woman out. Ruby has moved into the attic, so I'll fix up the bed in the guest room."

"That would be perfect."

Paisley's shift at the diner started in an hour. But if Sarah got upset or fearful when she dropped her off, she'd call in and explain that she'd be late. Bert would understand. Despite his boisterous voice and sometimes rowdy behavior, he was an understanding boss.

At the project house, Kathleen stood on the porch waiting as they exited the car. "Welcome, ladies."

"Hi, Kathleen! This is—"

Sarah gasped.

"What is it?" Paisley hurried over to her.

"This is ... this is where you're bringing me?" Eyes

bulging and face flushed, Sarah was obviously freaking out about something.

"Yes. Is something wrong?"

"I recognize this place. I mean, just barely. But—" Sarah covered her face with her hands and sobbed quietly.

"What's happened? What do you mean you recognize it?" Paisley put her arm over Sarah's shoulders and waited for her emotional breakdown to subside. "Are you okay?"

Kathleen approached them. "My dear, what's wrong?" She wrapped her arms around Sarah too. "There, there. What is it, sweetie?"

"This was ... my grandmother's house."

"Your grandmother's—?"

"You didn't know where Paisley was bringing you?" Kathleen asked. "This must be a shock."

"It is." Sarah wiped her eyes. "I was a little girl the last time we came here."

"Do you remember your grandmother's last name?" Surely, Sarah wasn't making this up, but considering all that happened to her recently, Paisley had to make sure.

"Peterson. Annie Peterson."

Paisley sighed. The property used to be called the Peterson place.

Kathleen tucked her hand into the crook of Sarah's arm and led her along the path. "Come along, dear. Let's get you situated. Then you can tell us all about it, hmm? Everything's going to be fine. You're safe here."

Feeling a little unsettled, Paisley followed behind them into the project house, then went up the stairs. Should she leave Sarah alone with Kathleen? Sarah recognizing the house seemed a little weird.

"When I first came to Basalt Bay, I didn't know anyone," Kathleen said in her soft voice as they crossed the hallway toward the guest room. "My mosaics and I moved into a tiny rental in town. Then I met Bess and Callie, and we jumped into buying this house together. Your grandparents' house?"

"Yes. I hardly recognize it, though."

"The place has been completely remodeled. Is that why you came to Basalt Bay? To see this house?" Kathleen asked in her gentle way.

Paisley was thankful for the older woman's mild prodding. She wanted some answers too.

"I'm heading north. Wandering, really." Sarah cleared her throat. "I thought I'd stop in Basalt Bay. I never expected to see my grandma's house looking so nice."

"Isn't it lovely?" Kathleen asked almost melodically.

Despite Sarah's sad features, a slight smile broke through and she nodded.

Kathleen helped remove her pack, then her coat. "This is a nice comfy bed." She fluffed the pillows and peeled back the top blanket, making the bed look cozy and inviting.

Sarah sat on the edge of the bed, her droopy gaze meeting Paisley's, then Kathleen's. She must be exhausted. Carrying the big backpack while hiking was enough to wipe out anyone, let alone sleeping on the beach, too.

"The bathroom is the next door over." Kathleen patted Sarah's shoulder.

"Are you okay?" Paisley got eye-level with Sarah. "I have to go to work, but you are safe here with Kathleen. She's a kind lady."

Sarah blinked slowly. "I can tell."

"We'll talk later, all right?"

"When you asked me to stay, I didn't know you meant here," she said in a small voice.

"I know."

"All of this is probably overwhelming." Kathleen shuffled toward the door. "How about if we leave you to settle in? Relax, if you want, or come downstairs for a cup of tea." She started to exit, then paused. "If you hear a clicking sound, I'm working on a mosaic project two doors down."

Sarah's eyes lit up. Then the gray shadow of despair or sadness washed over her face again.

"I'll talk to you later." Paisley waved, then followed Kathleen into the hallway. "Thank you for taking her in."

"Of course." Kathleen gave her a quick hug. "This is what the girls and I plan to do. I'm glad you brought her here. The poor dear looks like she could use some loving kindness in the world."

"I agree." Paisley shrugged. "I didn't know she had been in this house when she was a girl."

"But God knew. Isn't that beautiful? He led you to her right when she needed to be found."

Warmth flooded Paisley. "Yes, I think He did."

Twenty-seven

Ali had just put on her coat when the office door creaked open. The locals chose the worst times to pop in with mundane requests. "Can you put an article about my church bazaar in the paper?" "I lost my cat. Post a note in the classifieds, will you?" "Cancel my subscription!" What she needed was an assistant to field calls and unwanted visitors. Then maybe she'd have some peace and quiet to do her research and get the paper out on time.

"Going somewhere?"

Callie Cedars, again? What did she want this time?

"Yes, in fact, I am."

"Two days have passed, and I haven't seen an apology in the paper." The woman narrowed her eyes.

"You'll be waiting for the Pacific to freeze over before you read an apology from me. I told you—" Oh, what was the use? Ali buttoned up her coat. "Did you need something? I'm leaving for an appointment." To the salon in Florence, but no need to mention her nails were a disaster.

"I thought we might have another chat."

"I'll get my appointment book." Ali reached for the spiral notebook where she kept an abbreviated schedule.

"I have time right now. Got five minutes?"

Ali checked her phone. "Five minutes."

Callie leaned her hands against the counter and scowled. "Can't Milton afford a secretary to sort through this disaster?"

"Is that what you want to discuss? My uncle's messy office?" Ali tucked her cell phone into her coat pocket and took two steps toward the door.

"No. When are you going to write the article? Have you forgotten our arrangement?" Callie plopped a fist on her hip. "Perhaps, your memory needs jogging with another landslide of letters?"

"So, you were behind that? I won't be bullied into anything."

"Bullied?" Callie hooted. "You write a cruel article about my nephew-in-law, then you have the gall to say I'm bullying you?"

"My piece was based on facts. A source who—"

"What source?"

Ali unbuttoned and buttoned her coat again, hoping Callie got the hint. "I'm not at liberty to comment." Although, enough people had challenged her source that she was having doubts.

"You may not be able to comment, but I can. I will!" Callie thumped the counter surface with her knuckles. "I'd like a word with Milton today." She squinted around the room as if he might materialize.

"That won't be possible."

"Get him on the phone, then."

If only he would answer her calls.

"Your five minutes are up." Ali pointed toward the door. "Please, as I said, I have an appointment." When the other woman didn't budge, she asked with barely restrained patience, "Is there something else?"

"I'd like you to write your article before Christmas."

"You don't get to choose when I write anything." Who did this woman think she was?

Callie glared at her. "If you don't post an article saying you were misinformed, or whatever mumbo jumbo journalists use, before Christmas, our deal is off. You won't get any information from me."

"Fine. I won't be manipulated." Too bad she'd miss out on hearing Callie's viewpoint about Edward.

"You twist people's minds into believing what you say is truth, but you don't want to be manipulated?" Callie made a harsh-sounding laugh.

"I explore facts. Then I inform readers of my discoveries."

"Your twisted bias is as bad as Edward Grant's."

"That's absurd!"

"Is it?" Callie stared hard at her. "If you listened to less-than-stellar advice, you owe it to your readers to say so. They deserve the truth."

Ali opened her mouth to argue, wanting the last word, but nothing came out. Rarely lacking a comeback, her being flummoxed by Callie Cedars was odd. Yet the woman's words gnawed at her.

What if Uncle Milton's information came from an unreliable source? What if he was coerced into doing something he shouldn't have done? What if in telling her to write the article, he pulled her into whatever trouble he was in?

Twenty-eight

Forest sat on the couch with his laptop open, making a list of reasons he should pursue Mia's possible—probable, in his viewpoint—involvement in Edward's case, even if he had to do so on his own. First, unsolved cases drove him nuts. Second, he wanted to see justice done for Paisley. Then there were Mia's threats—maybe not viable—against him, Paige, and others. Her disobeying the no-contact rule with Edward still went unchallenged. Her flirty behavior, while not illegal, had seemingly been used to control people and get what she wanted. Perhaps, even with Deputy Brian.

Why didn't Sheriff Morris want Forest to pursue this angle anymore? Were his reasons due to a lack of funding? Or because of what Alison had written about him? Or was there something going on in this town he hadn't figured out yet?

In their last phone conversation, Sheriff Morris said, "Reports of Mia passing threats from Edward to citizens is unsubstantiated. More proof would be required for it to hold up in court. You know that."

Of course, he did. But what if he found out Mia was more involved in Edward's crimes than anyone realized? What if he was meant to discover more than he had so far? Was he willing to push for answers when Sheriff Morris and Deputy Brian weren't interested in pursuing anything against her? Did their lack of concern have anything to do with Edward? He highlighted the last question to ponder it some more.

This case was personal to him, too. After seeing that note from Evie to Edward about something happening on the night of the gala, he couldn't let the event take place. His wife's safety was reason enough for him to keep a watch on Mia's activity and get to the bottom of the insinuations.

He glanced across the room to the mantle filled with pictures of Piper, Paige, and Paul. He sighed, nostalgia filling him as it often did whenever he saw the cute photos of his daughter. If he'd been here two years ago when Piper was born, there'd be pictures of him and her on the mantle also. Maybe they'd take some Christmas photos of the three of them that could go up there.

Mentally shifting gears, he pondered the calls he needed to make while Paige was out of the house. He planned to call Mom, then his sister, Teal, to explain about the Christmas Eve surprise for Paige. He tapped "Mom" on his phone screen.

"Forest, honey, it's so good to hear from you."

He sighed, relaxing at hearing her voice. "Hey, Mom. How's it going?"

"Great. We're so excited to see you."

After a few minutes of pleasantries, he told her about his plans for the vow renewal ceremony on the beach. He cautioned her to keep the event a secret from Paige.

Mom cried and told him how pleased she was that he'd found happiness. And how she couldn't wait to meet Piper.

Next, he called Teal, who was two years younger than him. After their greetings, he asked, "Any chance Danson will be coming with you for the holidays?"

Mom had previously mentioned that Teal and Danson were temporarily separated, so Forest brought it up in case his sister wanted to talk about it.

"He's busy with his realtor responsibilities." Her tone turned sarcastic. "People buy houses at Christmastime, you know." She sighed. "The boys and I are looking forward to our visit. And I'm eager to meet my little niece."

"I can't wait to see you too, Sis. Say, do you mind if I give Danson a call?" Hopefully that didn't sound too pushy, but he cared about his brother-in-law also.

"I'd rather you didn't," she said stiffly. "Stay out of it, okay, Forest? He's living how he wants. I plan to do the same thing."

"All right." Maybe he shouldn't have mentioned anything.

"I might be moving down the coast," she said in a lighter tone. "The boys and I. Maybe we'll find a cute house and be neighbors with you."

"I'd love having you live closer to me." But did this mean she wasn't even planning to try to work things out with Danson?

"Wouldn't it be perfect for the boys and Piper to be close growing up?"

"It sure would. Any chance Danson would head this way with you?"

Deafening silence greeted him.

He cleared his throat. "Sorry. Not my business."

"No, it isn't." Teal made a swallowing sound. "While we're in Basalt Bay, I plan to look at options. Don't mention anything to Mom and Dad, okay? No need to worry them."

"Are you sure that's the wisest—"

"Forest, please. I'm an adult. I have two sons. I'm deciding what's best for us. Danson is, well, he's— Let's not have this discussion on the phone, okay?"

"Sure thing." A heaviness settled on his chest. He didn't like the thought of his sister going through the uncertainty and hurt of a divorce. He knew about that pain and confusion firsthand. Of course, he didn't know what struggles she might have already been going through. He'd make this a matter of prayer. "I'm here for you, no matter what."

"Thanks. I knew I could count on my big brother."

The call ended, but he felt heartsick about his sister's situation. His phone buzzed. Paisley's name popped up on his screen. He took a breath.

"Hey."

"Hi, Forest. Are you free to talk?"

"Sure. Paige is at the gallery."

"Good. I have some ideas for the ceremony at the gazebo. Want to hear my thoughts? Then you can decide the things you like best."

"Sounds good."

For the next ten minutes they batted around ideas about music, lanterns, and white fabric to wrap around the corners of the gazebo. Talking to his sister-in-law about the vow renewal got his thoughts whirling with possibilities, and away from the troubling discussion he had with Teal. Off his frustrations with Sheriff Morris's decision to not pursue Mia's possible involvement in Edward's crimes, too.

Forest had so many good things to look forward to in the days ahead—his family coming down from Portland, springing the vow renewal on Paige, and his first Christmas with her and Piper—that he shouldn't let any frustrations dominate his thoughts. But how could he let his suspicions about Mia go? The hunch he relied on as a private investigator, the one urging him to keep watching her until he found out the truth, told him to keep digging for answers.

He had to follow that nudge, didn't he?

Twenty-nine

The day after Paisley left Sarah in Kathleen's care, she dropped by the project house to check on her. "Good morning!" she said as she came through the front door.

"Paisley Rose, good to see you." Aunt Callie held up a plate of blueberry scones. "Hungry?"

"Sure am." Paisley felt hungrier than usual. Being extra hungry was a sign of pregnancy for her in the past. Did that mean something special now? What if she was just having fake symptoms? That happened sometimes, right? Especially when a woman wanted to be pregnant so badly. She hadn't experienced any morning sickness yet. No physical tenderness. So she still had doubts.

Paisley accepted the saucer Aunt Callie handed her. "Thanks. These look great."

"Kathleen made them for Sarah. Something to entice her to eat."

"She's not eating?" Was Sarah sick? Too troubled to eat?

"Not enough to keep a child alive." Aunt Callie tsk-tsked. "Poor thing."

Paisley bit into the pastry. "Mmm. This is good."

In between munching her treat, Callie continued, "She's withdrawn. Hasn't opened up to any of us. Kathleen told us about her being the granddaughter of the previous longtime owners of the house." Aunt Callie settled on the other stool, moving cautiously as if she were afraid it might tip over. "What an odd coincidence for you to run into her, huh?"

"Or providential." Paisley smiled. "A Christmas stranger? Room at the inn, and all that?"

"Hmm. You might be right."

"Where is Sarah? I was hoping to see her."

"Resting, I presume. She's mostly stayed in her room." Aunt Callie shook her head. "She didn't even come down for my chicken stew last night! I made it especially for her."

"Give her time. I'm so thankful you ladies had a place for her to stay. A lot of people wouldn't invite a homeless person into their house." Paisley brushed crumbs from her sweater. "There's something sad in her gaze, did you notice?"

Aunt Callie nodded. "That melancholy expression might mean she's suffering from trauma or grief."

"I used to see that look in my mirror every day. Maybe that's why I wanted to help her."

Aunt Callie hugged her. "I'm sorry for all you went through, Paisley Rose."

"Thank you, Auntie. If Sarah needs anything, you'll call me, won't you?"

"Sure, I will." Aunt Callie cleared her throat. "Heard anything from your dad? I haven't talked with him since Thanksgiving. We barely spoke then."

"He and Peter are making up for lost time." Paisley took

her plate to the kitchen sink. "I'm glad Peter will be here for Christmas."

"Me too. I'm looking forward to Christmas Eve dinner with all of us together."

"Same here." For the briefest second, Paisley had the urge to mention her secret. She longed to whisper to her aunt that next year they might have one more family member at the table. But she didn't want to disappoint Aunt Callie if her symptoms were a false alarm. And Judah should be the first person she told.

Lord, please let there be a baby growing inside me, she prayed for what felt like the hundredth time.

Thirty

After her appointment at the salon, Ali dropped onto a driftwood log near the trail's entrance to the beach. Craig texted her to meet him here, but why did he want to get together on the beach like this? Was he worried about her after that letter fiasco? If so, why? It wasn't like they were dating. He was someone from her past. Someone who held all his emotional pieces together with string and baling wire as well as she did.

She took a long draw of sea air. Since living in the city, she missed this. The moist air filled her lungs differently than recycled AC air ever could.

"Hey." Craig strode toward her, his hands stuffed into his jacket pockets. At least he didn't have on his fluorescent jail vest today. Although his swagger and good looks—things she was attracted to—were still in place.

"Good afternoon."

He dropped onto the log beside her. Not too close. But this setting of them being alone on the beach, no one else in sight, felt intimate and secluded like they were the only two people in the world. She wanted to shuffle to the far right edge of the log, putting more space between them, protecting her heart. But she didn't. If she moved away, he might think she didn't trust him. When really, it was herself she didn't trust.

"Why did you want to meet with me?" Did her voice go soft? Just an overreaction to being close to him?

A slow smile crossed his mouth as if he knew the power he had over her. "Are you in a hurry to get away from me?"

"No." Yes, she internally amended. "I'm a busy woman." A career-minded woman who had to get back to work. One who needed to keep her distance from Craig, too. "What do you want?"

One of his eyebrows pulsed upward.

Her cheeks burned. What did a man like him usually want other than flirtation when he met a woman alone on the beach?

Hmm. A little harmless flirting might be fun.

Her core heated up at the thought of their lips pressing together softly. Of their arms wrapped around each other in a close embrace. She silenced a groan. Why was she even considering Craig Masters as a romantic interest? Too bad he didn't wear his bright green vest today! If he had, she'd be able to manage her thoughts better.

"So? What is it?"

Craig stared toward the incoming waves. "What are you doing on Christmas Eve?"

"What?" Of any question he might have asked her, that was the last one she would have guessed.

His smiling lips drew her attention to them. He had such a nice smile.

"You know the holiday where people sit around eating too much sugar and singing ridiculous songs?"

"You celebrate Christmas?" Her voice shot up.

"Don't I look like a guy who celebrates Christmas?"

"You seem more like—"

"Like what?" His smile vanished.

"More the Scrooge type."

Craig belted out a laugh. "You might be correct. But I got an invitation for Christmas Eve dinner. I thought I'd see if your being my plus-one might be in the stars."

"Like a date?"

A less cocky look crossed his face. "It could happen. A man and a woman find each other attractive"—he winked at her—"and meet up for dinner at someone's house."

"Whose house?"

"It's a Grant/Cedars bash."

"You've got to be kidding!" She tucked her coat around her knees so the wind wouldn't upend the hem of her dress. "You're going to eat with them? Cozy up and sing 'Jingle Bells' around the campfire?"

"Is sitting around a campfire a thing people do on Christmas?" Craig snorted. "So you're not interested, then?"

She pelted him with a glare. "Did you forget the article I wrote? Forest Harper is part of that family. I had visits from his wife and her aunt. Do you imagine I'd sit across the dinner table from them? How fake do you think I am?"

She lunged to her feet. Only her heels caught in the sand, and she was suddenly propelled forward, falling, her hands flailing. Craig grabbed hold of her, steadying her, his hands tender as he drew her against his torso and held her until she got her footing.

"You okay?" he asked huskily.

"Uh, yeah. Thanks." Her face felt like it heated up five times worse than usual.

Imagining herself sagging against him, kissing his cheek to show her gratitude, she pushed away. None of that. She was in Basalt Bay for one reason—to fill in for her uncle. Until he returned, she'd keep digging up information on the Grants. Eating at their table, the enemies' table, for Christmas Eve? No way in a million years.

"Thank you for the invitation, but I can't be your dinner date for Christmas Eve." She shuffled through the sand back to the trail, cursing her choice in shoes.

Not far behind her, Craig's voice reached her, "How about having lunch with me?"

She whirled around. "Now?"

"Why not?" His black hair blew in the breeze, his usual smirk in place. "Then I can try to persuade you to change your mind."

For a heartbeat, she considered telling him to get lost. But she liked being with Craig Masters. What would it hurt to eat lunch with him?

Thirty-one

Her shoulder muscles tensing up, Paisley approached the next table in her section where a familiar older woman sat. Maggie Thomas. Why today? While the proverbial hatchet had been buried between them during Bess's election, Paisley felt a cooling in the woman's attitude ever since she returned to work at Bert's. "What can I get for you this afternoon, Mrs. Thomas?" she asked in her sweetest server's voice.

The innkeeper stared intensely at the menu, not looking up. "How's the salmon burger?"

"Great, as always. I had one yesterday with avocado. It's my favorite."

"I'll take one of those. Skip the fries." She patted her waistline. "I'll have the salad."

"Got it." Paisley scribbled on the ordering pad.

"How's that homeless woman doing out at Callie's?" Maggie scraped her fingernail against a mark on the table surface. "If you ask me, it's a dangerous scheme. Opening one's home to strangers is risky. I warned your aunt she was off her rocker to consider it."

"Sarah seems like a nice person, just down on her luck." Like I was, she almost added.

Maggie scowled. "Are you going to get my sandwich, or do I have to make it myself?"

"I'll get this order started." Agitation churning in her middle, Paisley rushed across the diner. Maggie could make her good day turn bad faster than anyone!

She hooked the order on the circular ordering queue and gave it a shove. The door jangled and she turned in case someone needed directions to a table. Craig and Alison strolled in smiling at each other. Were they a couple? The way Craig's hand rested at Alison's back, and the way he gazed at her tenderly, looked like he thought of them as a couple.

A breath caught in Paisley's throat. A painful flashback of Craig forcing a kiss on her breached her thoughts. *Grace and mercy,* she repeated Judah's mantra, hoping it helped. Taking a deep breath, making sure her airways were clear, she grabbed two menus and followed the duo toward the back. Thank goodness they didn't choose the kissing booth.

Craig's gaze pinned hers. He nodded once.

She forced herself to offer a slight smile. This man was her husband's brother, after all. He had assisted her father during a life-threatening crisis. Helped with her rescue. May have saved her life. They were family now.

She and Judah had been praying for Craig every day since finding out the DNA results. Perhaps, this was her chance to show him God's love, mercy, and forgiveness. Then why did she feel so tongue-tied? *Lord, help me.* Gulp. *Help!*

Since his release from jail, Craig had been in the diner

several times. But Lucy usually took his order. Paisley was spared the ordeal. Until now.

"Paisley," he mumbled.

Alison glanced up sharply.

"What can I get for you two?" Paisley set a menu in front of each of them. "Coffee?"

"That would be great," Craig answered.

"Earl Gray, if you have it, with hot water," Alison said in a clipped tone like she was telling a teenager what to do.

"Coming right up." Paisley rushed away quicker than she usually departed from customers' tables.

Eventually, she'd have to deal with having a real conversation with Craig. First, she needed time to figure out how to behave with a man she was so afraid of in the past. With God's love working in her heart, that should get easier. Hadn't she agreed with Judah about inviting him to Christmas Eve dinner? She might have to speak with him then.

Hands trembling, she filled the drink order and buzzed them back to Craig and Alison. Setting both drinks on their table without spilling a drop took all her concentration.

"Thanks," Craig said quietly.

"Oh, Paisley—"

Too bad she didn't rush away quicker.

"Yes?" She drew the ordering pad out of her apron in case Alison was ready to order. "Breaded salmon is today's special."

"That's fine. I wondered"—the woman pulsed her pinkish manicured fingernails over her hair as if checking for stray locks—"if you'd be willing to have a chat with me."

"A chat?" Paisley glanced between the two. "About?"

"Your alleged kidnapping."

"Alleged?" Paisley's heart rate accelerated.

Craig cleared his throat. "Al—"

"I don't mean to bring up a touchy subject. It's an honest request for an interview. You'd get the chance to share your side of the story."

Her side? Did she mean Paisley's story might not be the official story?

"I don't think she wants to—"

"No, that won't be possible. The case hasn't gone to court yet." Paisley swallowed hard. "I'll be back for your order in a second."

She ran all the way to the kitchen, not caring if she made a spectacle of herself. Tears flooded her eyes. Why was she being so emotional today?

Behind the swinging doors, the sounds of pans being washed, the dishwasher going, and voices clamoring with orders overrode her heart pounding in her ears. She scrambled to the farthest corner in the room, then leaned over the garbage can and drew deep breaths in and out, counting them. *One. Breathe. Two. Breathe.* She hadn't experienced such a strong internal reaction to someone in weeks.

Relax. No one's going to harm you. God is with you.

"Paisley?" Bert tapped her shoulder.

She jumped. Gulping, she wiped her fingers beneath her eyes, hoping she hadn't smeared her mascara.

"Did something happen? Are you okay?" He peered at her intensely.

"I'll be fine. Oh, wait." A big swallow. "Could Zoe take Table Ten, please? Just this time?" She hated the desperate sound in her voice. But right then, she felt desperate.

Bert twisted the tips of his mustache to fine points. "Who's at Table Ten?"

He didn't like anyone requesting a switch for table assignments. When Paisley took the job here again, she knew this might be a problem. That she'd be expected to serve whoever sat down in her section. Today, that meant Craig and Alison.

"Never mind. I'll, um, take care of it."

"You sure you're okay?"

"Give me ten seconds, and I will be." Or maybe ten hours.

He started to walk away, paused. "If you need to talk, I have two ears."

"Thanks, Bert."

It took quite a few more breaths and a personal lecture— *You can do this. Don't look Craig in the eye! Don't agree to anything with the journalist*—before she pulled herself together enough to bring Maggie her plate of food and then stop by Craig's table to take their order.

"What'll it be?" That was probably abrupt. But she didn't want to make small talk. She poised a pen over her pad, not making eye contact with either of them.

"Bacon burger for me." Craig tapped his fingers in a drumbeat against the table surface.

"Paisley—"

"Just the order, please." She interrupted Alison, keeping her voice modulated, not giving into the emotions boiling below the surface. She had a job to do, without having a breakdown or a panic attack. "The breaded salmon?"

"Yes, thank you." Alison sighed.

"I'll get this order in." Paisley scooped up the menus. "Ready for a refill?"

Craig didn't answer, so she met his gaze. He mouthed, "Sorry."

Sighing, she nodded, then moved away from the danger zone. At the kitchen window, she snapped the order into the wheel.

That hadn't been so bad. Right. More like a harrowing calamity! But the first time doing anything difficult was the worst. Serving Craig and Alison should get easier, right?

Thirty-two

Craig glared across the table at Al. He may have made a drastic mistake in inviting her to the Christmas Eve dinner. "What were you thinking?"

"What do you mean?" She dipped her tea bag up and down in the steaming water, adding a spoon of sugar and stirring.

"Why did you badger Paisley?"

"Badger?" Ali brought the cup to her red lips and sipped. "I'm a reporter. I ask questions. Report the news."

"She isn't the news."

"Are you her champion now? By what I've heard, you two are—" She shrugged inconclusively.

"Are what?"

"Enemies, if the gossips have the story correct."

So she was checking up on him? Pestering Paisley? Craig clenched his jaw.

He caught a few harsh glances coming from some of the locals in the diner. Maggie Thomas pelted him with an evil eye. She'd better not come by his table today.

"Are you?" One of Al's penciled eyebrows rose dramatically.

"Am I what?"

"Her enemy?" Her tone changed into a playful lilt. "Or ex-lovers?"

"No," he said gruffly. "Never that."

"But you wanted it to be so?"

Man, he didn't need her prying into his life. He ground his teeth together. Gulped down a wash of coffee. "Just leave her alone, will you?"

"Can't make promises I won't keep. I'm sniffing out a story before it becomes yesterday's news." She sipped her drink and gazed at him like she had him all figured out.

"When are you leaving town?"

"Eager for me to go?"

"The reporter in you? Maybe." He shuffled his shoulders that were tired from his bending over and picking up junk in the back lot behind Lewis's Super. "The sharp-witted beautiful woman sitting across from me? I'd like her to stay for a long time, if she wasn't so prickly."

"Prickly? What about the mile-wide chip on your shoulder? Will it ever dissipate?"

"I doubt it." He decided to change the subject. "Have you thought any more about coming to Christmas Eve dinner with me?"

"In the last half hour?" She glanced across the room. "With Paisley unwilling to talk to me, and you sticking up for her, you expect me to sit nicely at Christmas dinner and keep my mouth shut?" She gave him a wide-eyed look. "You're something else, Craig."

"I'll take that as a compliment."

"Take it as you like. The answer's still no."

Without speaking, Paisley set a plate with a burger and fries in front of him. She did the same with Al's salmon plate. Then she rushed off without talking. He swallowed a knot of regret in his throat.

Al tilted her head, staring at him as if peering into his brain. "On second thought, sitting at a Cedars and Grant holiday hoopla might be the exact place where I could get the information I need for my article."

"Al—"

She tossed him a smirky expression.

He bit back a groan. What could he say? He could hardly uninvite her now.

Thirty-three

In the three days since Ruby told him she didn't want to see him, Peter had abided by her no-contact rule. Although tempted to call her hourly, not storming over to the project house and demanding to see her took every bit of willpower and patience he possessed. He needed to try again to explain how much he loved her and wanted to be with her and that he hadn't meant anything offensive by his words.

But how dare she accuse him of being romantic with her just to get her to move back to the boat with him! How dare she act like he'd done nothing to prove his love to her! He left his troller. Came to Basalt Bay. Lived with his dad to give her space. Why couldn't she see the sacrifices he'd made for her? Why weren't they enough?

Taking long strides, he hiked along the beachfront, heading out to Judah and Paisley's cabin south of town. He'd called ahead and asked to speak with Judah. He was desperate to talk to someone.

How was he going to prove anything to Ruby when she refused to see him? Maybe he should head back to Ketchikan. He groaned. No, he didn't want to do that. After he tried everything he could possibly do to reach Ruby's heart, and if she still didn't want to return north with him, then he'd have to face facts. Not yet.

As he trekked along the shoreline, he breathed in deeply of the sea air, letting the coolness fill him. The peace of it, if only for a few minutes.

Up ahead, Judah stood in front of his beach house with a cup in his hand. He waved and Peter returned the gesture.

The male-bonding talk he figured he'd have with his brother-in-law would probably be like pulling teeth. Never good at sharing personal stuff, Peter had reached the end of his tether. If anyone could understand marital exasperation, it had to be Judah. Didn't he wait three years for Paisley to come home? Three years! Peter couldn't imagine that.

"Hey, man." Judah shook his hand. "Great afternoon for a beach walk, huh?"

"Sure is." Peter stood by him and faced the waves rolling in. "What a view you guys have."

"We're blessed. I can't imagine living anywhere else."

"That's how I feel about my boat." Peter stuck his hands in his jacket pockets.

"You must miss living on the sea. Have you gotten your land legs yet?"

"Sure. But I miss being on my boat tremendously."

"I bet. Want some coffee?" Judah held up his cup.

"No, thanks." He rarely turned down his favorite drink,

but with the inner struggle he felt, even coffee didn't sound appetizing.

Judah set his cup down in the sand. "You said you wanted to talk?"

"Yeah." Peter swallowed a behemoth gulp.

They stood in silence. A seagull made a big racket swooping down and snatching something from the beach before another bird got to it.

"So, what's going on?" Judah asked. "Are things getting any better between you and Ruby?"

"Things were improving, or so I thought. Then the walls came crashing down again." Peter scuffed the sole of his hiking boot against the sand. "Women, huh?"

"I doubt the problem is with the women."

"No?" Peter said in a scoffing tone. "Why not?"

"I'd say it's our male stubbornness and pride that gets us into trouble."

"Hey, you're supposed to be on my side."

"I'm on both your sides." Judah clapped Peter's shoulder. "I like Ruby too."

"Yeah, yeah. Everyone likes her," he said grumpily. "She's got a stubborn streak, too."

"I don't doubt it. So does my wife."

"Not Paisley!" Peter said in mock disbelief.

Judah snickered. After a moment, he got serious again. "Ruby loved you and married you. Stayed married to you, even when things weren't going so well, right?"

"Yeah." Peter waited for the ax to fall.

"Even when she could have gotten a divorce, she didn't."

The word "divorce" branded itself hot and painful in his chest.

"But she left me."

"Yes. She came looking for your family. Somewhere you could find her."

Peter drew in a long breath. "Doesn't make getting back together any easier."

"No. Reconciliation can be tough. It happens in stages. Baby steps." Judah nodded toward the beach and with a slow gait, walked farther south.

Peter caught up with him, veering around a pile of sand.

"So what brings you here today?" Judah asked. "Other than the great ocean view."

"She says she wants me to prove myself worthy."

"Oh?"

"Not worthy, exactly. More like I'm supposed to prove my love. Prove something. I don't know what she expects." Another painful sensation burned in his chest.

"I see."

"You do? I can hardly understand what she wants myself."

"Perhaps she's looking for something in you she hasn't felt." Judah shrugged a couple of times. "Asking you to prove yourself doesn't mean she doesn't love you."

"We're at a stalemate."

A bird cawed in a nearby tree. A motorboat chugged noisily through the bay. They walked in silence for a ways down the beach.

"What's the next step?" Judah asked.

"Beats me. Thus my call to talk with you. Any suggestions?" Peter bent over and picked up a rock, smoothing it in his hand. "She doesn't want us to see each other until I do whatever it is she wants me to do. Her making the rules and saying I can't see her drives me nuts! What am I? A school-boy?"

"You're obviously upset and worried. Maybe offended?"

"Wouldn't you be?"

"I would." Judah chuckled. "Grace is a funny thing, though."

"Funny how?" Peter tossed the rock into the waves.

"I mean, if we honestly have grace for other people's mistakes, shouldn't we have grace for our spouse? Even for ourselves?"

Peter scratched his scalp. "I hadn't thought about it."

"Why did you want to talk with me?" Judah paused mid-step. "I mean, I'm glad you texted. You're welcome here anytime. But you could have talked about this with Forest or your dad."

Peter barked out a laugh. "Dad has a code for what men can talk about. How they should behave. 'Make peace at any cost.'" He exaggerated Dad's voice. "But Ruby balked at my efforts to try to make her happy. Isn't her happiness at the helm of her demand that I prove myself?"

"Maybe." Judah continued walking. "Have you tried apologizing for whatever broke you guys up?"

"I did."

"Have you talked about it? Gotten seriously humble and open?"

Peter didn't like the sound of that. "Somewhat."

"She probably needs more honest discussions from you," Judah said in a way that felt less intimidating. "For Paisley and me it took a few heartfelt, and awkward, talks. Not just one simple discussion."

"I hate talking about stuff like that. Even mentioning this to you is gut awful."

"I understand." Judah play punched him in the arm. "You didn't answer why you called me, but I'm guessing it's because of what your sister and I went through."

"Yeah." Peter toed a rock and sent it skidding along the sand. "I thought you'd have a different perspective on it."

"Getting real and honest with your wife can be the hardest thing you do." Judah took a deep breath. "But it's worth it. Are you hearing what I'm saying?"

"I have to be honest with Ruby?"

"And seriously mean it. Cause if you're faking it, she'll know."

Peter learned that the hard way. "What about proving my love? What does she want? Five dozen roses? A diamond ring?" The ruby he purchased in Alaska flashed through his thoughts. He doubted jewelry would prove anything to his wife.

"Ask her."

"She isn't speaking to me."

"Is there anything you've been holding back on? Something the two of you have argued about? Hurt feelings, maybe?"

"What did she say to you?"

"Nothing. What do you think she said to me?"

"I don't know."

"Yes, you do. Something obviously came to mind." Judah grinned.

What was so humorous?

"She called my boat my mistress."

"Ouch."

"Exactly. She asked if we could get a house, and I refused." Peter clicked his fingers. "Would buying a house prove my love to her? Make her want to come back to Alaska with me?"

"As nice as buying a house might sound, proving your love goes deeper than that."

Groaning, Peter scraped his hands through his hair. "I wish I knew what she wants."

"You might try praying. I don't know where you stand with your faith. But if it was me, and my wife didn't want to talk with me, I'd be on my knees praying about it." Judah placed one hand over his heart. "That grace I was talking about earlier? It's been a life-changer for me. Paisley, too. If we have grace for everyone, including our spouse and ourselves, what past sin or flaw can we hold against anyone?"

Peter felt rooted to the spot. Frozen in place as if he couldn't move forward until he had an answer to Judah's question. Yet he lacked any answers having to do with spiritual things.

Was he holding onto something from his past? Maybe something that had grown in him like an emotional cancer? What had the clerk in the souvenir shop back in Ketchikan said? Ruby went looking for the source of his pain. Where did that pain begin, if not within himself?

Thirty-four

His fingers poised over his laptop in his makeshift office in the kitchen, Forest typed out the questions he'd like to ask Mia. *What do you know about the threat concerning the gallery? Were any of the things you told people that supposedly came from Edward true? What do you get out of being Edward's voice to the community?*

Was she seeking power? Had Edward promised her a governmental position if she did what he asked? Surely, she was after something. Money. Prestige. Respect. What kind of bond did she have with the ex-mayor to risk being arrested herself? Maybe she thought she was above the law. Did that have anything to do with her relationship with Deputy Brian?

Thoughts Forest previously entertained about the deputy's involvement with Mia were compounded by what he recently overheard about them dating. Did Brian's interest in Mia blind him to her faults?

Enough questions. It was time for some answers!

Forest picked up his cell phone and called Mia's phone number, but it went straight to voicemail. He tried four more times with the same result. Should he leave a message? Even "Call me," might be construed as inappropriate. He ended his last attempt to reach her cell. Maybe she had to silence her phone during work hours. He tapped his screen for the C-MER number.

A nasally voice he didn't recognize answered. "Hello. Basalt Bay C-MER. Betsy Tomkins speaking. How may I direct your call?"

"Uh." Forest cleared his throat. "I had a question for the receptionist. Is she there?"

"That would be me today," Betsy said. "How can I help you?"

"Is Mia Till gone for the day?"

"That's right."

"Is she expected in tomorrow?" He kept his tone polite, knowing he was pushing the lines of privacy by asking.

"I can't give out that information. What did you need assistance with?"

"I'll call back. Thanks." Forest ended the connection.

Mia wasn't answering her phone and she wasn't at work today? Hmm.

He tapped Brian's number.

"Yeah?" the deputy answered, sounding bored.

"I was hoping to speak with Mia." Forest strode across the kitchen, his cell phone snug against his ear. "Any idea where she might be?"

"No. Why do you wish to speak with her? You're off the case, remember?"

"I know." How many times was Deputy Brian going to

remind him of that? "How about Evie? Do you mind if I come by and have a chat with her?"

"She can receive visitors, if she wants to see them." Brian snorted. "I doubt she'd agree to talk with you."

Since he was off the case, he couldn't push for that to happen, either.

"Did you talk with her?"

"About?" Brian dragged out the word.

"The threat concerning the gallery event?"

"Yes, but she wouldn't give me a straight answer. I passed the letter I intercepted on to Sheriff Morris." Brian inhaled noisily. "Is that it?"

"Yeah. That's it."

Feeling like he struck out on all fronts, Forest returned to the table and searched a couple more leads via the internet. If he couldn't get to the bottom of the threat concerning the gala, Paige wasn't going to be able to proceed with her plans for a grand event in the new year. That wasn't going to sit well with her, but it couldn't be helped.

With the holidays upon them, and the trial approaching, he felt an urgency to get these unsolved issues figured out.

Thirty-five

With three days until Christmas Eve, Paisley arranged for a planning meeting at the project house with Bess, Callie, Ruby, and Kathleen. She wanted them to put their heads together to figure out how to make their holiday dinner and the surprise vow renewal afterward spectacular.

She also wanted to check on Sarah.

The five ladies sat around the long dining room table that would accommodate twelve adults for their special meal. Another table would have to be set up for the rest of the group.

This Christmas would be a celebration of firsts—the ladies' first Christmas in the project house. Paisley and Judah's first Christmas back together. Forest and Paige's too.

She smoothed her hand over her flat stomach. Possibly, her first Christmas with a secret to announce.

"What's our tally?" Aunt Callie asked. "Is Pauly coming?"

"Yes, he is." Paisley busied her hands with folding and unfolding a napkin. Dad and Aunt Callie at the same table?

She and Craig? What about Alison? Would she be Craig's dinner date? Cringe. "Craig might be coming. And his plus-one."

"What?" Aunt Callie's voice went shrill. "That you invited him turns my stomach."

"Now, now," Bess said. "God's love compels us to do unusual deeds sometimes."

"You're okay with this?" Callie gawked at her. "Having your ex's son at the dining room table with you on Christmas Eve?"

"I didn't say it would be easy." Bess chuckled. "But, yes, I'm okay with Judah inviting his brother to join us for dinner. The two of them need to make amends and work things out. They'll be brothers for the rest of their lives. Adjustments have to be made by all."

"Paisley Rose," Aunt Callie said sternly. "Are you okay with the man who caused you so much heartache coming here and bringing his date along with him?"

"Isn't that what forgiveness is?" Paisley scrunched the napkin tighter. "Aren't we supposed to extend mercy and grace?"

Aunt Callie muttered something under her breath.

"I, for one, applaud Bess and Paisley's decision to love this man, no matter what he did," Kathleen said in a soft voice. "What does the verse say? 'Love covers over a multitude of sins.' Isn't that wonderful?"

"Amen," Bess said.

"Well, I think—"

"Auntie," Paisley interrupted her, "let's get on with the logistics of our gathering, shall we? My count is seventeen adults, including Sarah, Craig and his guest, Forest's parents and sister, James, and all of us. Oh, and three kids."

"James?" Callie asked in a high-pitched voice. "Who invited him?"

"Dad." Paisley lifted her chin. "You wouldn't leave James home alone to celebrate Christmas Eve by himself, would you?"

"Why not? He has ignored—" Aunt Callie pursed her lips. "Never mind."

"Callie, we could use more hungry, single men around here," Kathleen said in a teasing tone.

The other ladies chuckled.

Aunt Callie stared out the window as if disinterested in the conversation now. Was she that upset about James Weston coming to dinner? Here Paisley thought she liked Dad's neighbor!

"We can put up a folding table there." Bess pointed to the opposite side of the room. "Twelve at this table, five adults and the kids over there. Cozy, but it should work."

"I can't wait for all of us to cook together in our kitchen." Kathleen clapped her hands. "Christmas music playing. Us baking our favorite holiday recipes. We have those long countertops and the island. Plenty of space for prepping a big family meal."

"Sounds like a blast!" Bess said.

"I'm sure Paige will want to help too," Paisley added.

"Why isn't she here then?" Aunt Callie asked in an offended tone.

"I didn't invite her."

"Paisley Rose—"

"Not because I didn't want to include her. I need to talk to you ladies about something without her being here. It's a secret Judah and I and Forest have drummed up."

She quickly explained about the surprise vow renewal on the beach.

The ladies oohed and aahed.

"What would you like us to do?" Ruby spoke up. "How can we help?"

"I'm glad you asked." Paisley smiled at her sister-in-law who'd been quiet up to this point. She knew Peter talked with Judah yesterday, but she didn't know what their conversation was about. Although she could guess. "We need to come up with some simple decorations and lighting we can put up at the gazebo on Christmas Eve. Any ideas?"

"Lanterns," Ruby offered. "Or flashlights."

"How about solar lighting like you use for yards or gardens?" Kathleen asked.

"That sounds good," Paisley said. "Easy to set up and take down."

"How about a bonfire?" Ruby suggested. "That would light up the night sky."

"True. We have three days. Let's come up with some easy ways to decorate and put up folding chairs in the sand, or maybe blanket seating." Paisley put her index finger to her mouth in a shushing gesture. "Remember, it's a secret. No spilling the beans to Paige."

"I don't know about traipsing to and from the beach in this cold weather," Aunt Callie said grumpily. "Why don't they have their ceremony in the church? Easier for me to get to."

"Sorry, Auntie. If you want to come to this shindig, you'll have to traipse out to the gazebo with the rest of us."

"What about Craig and his date?" Aunt Callie plucked at her sweater. "Where will they sit for dinner? How about if we put them at their own table in the living room?"

"Callie!" Kathleen exclaimed. "It's Christmastime. Remember about spreading goodwill?"

Aunt Callie harrumphed.

As soon as the ladies finished discussing food ideas, Paisley slipped away to check on Sarah. She tapped on her bedroom door.

"Come in."

Paisley opened the door. "Hello. I want to check on how you are doing. Is everything going okay?"

"It sure is nice here," Sarah spoke softly from the chair where she sat with a blanket over her shoulders. "Your kindness means a great deal to me."

"I'm glad my aunt and my mother-in-law had a room where you could rest and be warm." Paisley noticed Sarah's backpack on the floor near the end of the bed. "You will be staying for Christmas, won't you?"

"It seems like such an intrusion."

"It's not. Believe me. You are welcome here for as long as you want to stay." Paisley leaned against the doorframe, shuffling her right slip-on shoe against the tiling. "It may be chaotic on Christmas Eve, fair warning. But I'd love for you to be here with us."

"Thank you."

She didn't know the cause of Sarah's sadness, but the

downhearted emotions were there on her face, evident in the droop of her shoulders.

Lord, please touch this woman. Help her through whatever problem she's going through.

"Is there anything you need? Anything I can get for you while I'm here?"

"I'm good. Thanks."

"All right. Let me know. Or talk to Ruby or Kathleen."

"I will."

Sarah's face was so pale. Was she sick? What had happened to her?

Thirty-six

Paige took the broom outside and swept the sidewalk in front of the gallery like she usually did each morning. Even though the weather was cool, the street along the ocean-side had a regular influx of dirt. Sometimes a pile of sand accumulated in the corners of the entrance, and she had to sweep it a couple of times a day to keep the grains from wandering inside.

The thud, thud, thud of heels approaching fast made her spin around.

Blond hair tucked behind her ears, hands deep inside the pockets of her trench coat, Alison headed toward her like she was on a mission. She wasn't someone Paige wanted to see this morning. But a potential customer, nonetheless.

Paige hurried inside and set the broom in the closet. Nervously, she went to her position behind the coffee shop counter. Alison was probably coming in for a hot drink. Not to chat or discuss the letters.

"Good morning," Alison said, withdrawing a wallet from her coat pocket. "A tall Americana, please."

"Of course." Paige made the financial transaction, cutting glances at the woman in profile.

Gold dangling earrings hung from Alison's ears, almost brushing her collar. Her sober expression was aimed toward Paige's nook of paintings. Did she hate them? With such a scowl, it was hard to read her. The artwork obviously wasn't eliciting a happy response.

"I've been contemplating the letter I might write for the paper." Paige decided to break the ice between them.

"Good. I have space in tomorrow's edition."

"Oh. You do?" Gulp. She hadn't anticipated writing one so quickly. Maybe she should tell Alison never mind.

"I'd need it by three o'clock today."

"Today? Oh, uh, okay." Paige finished prepping the order, then slid the drink toward Alison. "If things remain quiet around here, I could probably write something." Now, why did she agree to that?

"Fine." A gleam in her eye, Alison said, "Did you hear Craig invited me to Christmas Eve with your family?"

"He did?" Paige's voice came out like a yelp.

Having Craig at the same table with Paisley and Judah, even with her and Forest, would be weird enough. Now, Alison might be there, too?

"Surprises you, huh?"

"Yeah. Sort of." She forced herself to say the next words calmly, and to mean them, "But you'd be welcome. It's Christmas. A time of peace." She swallowed hard.

"Hmm. I wonder." Alison sipped her drink.

"Tell Craig hello. We're friends."

"I know about you and Craig. What I'm curious about is him and Paisley. What's their history?" One of Alison's eyebrows tilted high as if asking Paige to fill in the details. "He's tightlipped, as you can imagine."

"That's our Craig." Paige pressed her lips together to show Alison she wasn't confiding anything in her, either.

"I'll let you get to your writing." Alison moved toward the door. "See you at three." Then she was gone.

Paige groaned. Why did she have to go and bring up the newspaper piece? Maybe the gallery would fill up with so many customers, she'd be too busy to write anything.

Thirty-seven

Sitting at the table in the planning room, Ruby picked up a photo of a man in a dapper hat, dressed in a suit coat and tie. His arm was around a lovely lady who wore a white dress. Although, since they were black and white photos, it could just as easily have been a pink or yellow dress. Both wore wide smiles. Their wedding day?

A throat clearing sound drew Ruby's attention away from the photo.

"Oh, Sarah," she said to the woman in the doorway. "Hello."

"I didn't know you were in here."

"That's okay. Would you like to look at some old pictures with me?"

"I don't want to intrude."

"You won't be intruding. Come on in."

In the two days since Sarah arrived, Ruby hadn't heard her say more than a few words. Now, she entered the room looking rosier cheeked and more alert. Maybe she felt better.

"I found these photographs in the attic. Kathleen told me about your family connection to this house. Do you think you might recognize any of the people?" Ruby held up a picture. "Like this pony with a girl on it who looks to be seven or eight. Care to take a guess at who she is?"

"I was young when we left Basalt Bay." Sarah shuffled forward. "It's probably my grandmother. I dreamed of having a pony when I was a kid." She dropped into a folding chair and sighed like talking wore her out.

"When I was a girl, I wanted to ride a whale." Ruby chuckled.

Sarah cracked a grin. In a blink, it was gone. But for that moment, Ruby captured a glimpse of happiness in the woman's otherwise taut expression.

Sarah picked up one of the more damaged photos.

"Do you recognize anyone?"

"No. What were you going to do with these before I showed up?"

"I hoped to find an address." Ruby picked up another photo and stared intently at a boy in the entryway of a barn. "Do you have any relatives who might want these photos? Jennifer Richards is your mom, right? I saw her name on the property ledger."

"She passed away five years ago."

"Oh. I'm sorry."

"She didn't want anything to do with Grandma's house. I never knew why." Sarah took in a slow breath. "I have a brother. But he doesn't care about our past in Basalt Bay. He's wealthy. Never called after—" She shook her head as if she said too much.

"Maybe you'd like these." Ruby nudged a pile of photos toward her. "Why don't you sort through them? Something might ring a bell."

An hour later, Kathleen entered the planning room. "You girls must have been up early."

"We got a head start sorting through these photos." Ruby spread her hands toward the piles she and Sarah had already combed through. "We're not in your way, are we?"

"Not at all. Do you mind if I work at my table?"

"Go right ahead."

"Morning, Sarah," Kathleen said softly.

"Good morning." Sarah smiled at the other woman then returned her gaze to the photo in her hands.

Kathleen nodded at Ruby, her eyes shimmering, as if silently thanking her for including Sarah in this project.

The photos were of Sarah's family, but she seemed comfortable with Ruby. Maybe because she was the youngest of the ladies living in the project house. Or because she, too, was in a place of struggle in her life.

Was that obvious in her eyes also?

Thirty-eight

Enjoying the serenity and quiet of her early morning painting time, Paige perused the canvas she was working on as a surprise for Bess, Aunt Callie, and Kathleen. So far, her rendering of their remodeled house, with rays of sunshine bathing the roof in sunlight and a bit of ocean peeking through the trees on both sides of the building, was coming along nicely. The painting wouldn't be finished by Christmas, but soon after the new year it should be done.

She still hadn't faced the task of touching up her lighthouse picture. One of these mornings, she'd have to try to repair whatever damage Piper's juice spill caused. She still got a glug in her throat every time she imaged the moment when she thought her painting was ruined. Thankfully, that wasn't the case.

Today, something other than wanting to paint prompted her to get up early. Her letter to the editor was probably in the paper, and Peter was going to bring Dad's copy by.

How would Forest take the news of her submission? Would he understand she was trying to be supportive of him by writing the letter? Or would he think she went behind his back and did what he didn't want her to do? She'd hate for this to be their first argument since their marriage, especially two days before Christmas Eve. She felt so strongly she couldn't sit back and do nothing. However, her timing might have been all wrong.

"Morning." Forest's bare feet padded across the floor behind her.

She set her paintbrush down on the easel ledge then turned to meet his lips for a good-morning kiss. He held her close, and she clung to him. *Lord, help him be okay with what I did.* Maybe she should tell him about the letter before the paper arrived.

A quiet tap came at the front door.

Too late.

"Who's—"

"It's Peter."

"What's he doing here this early?"

"Tell you in a sec." Worrying her lower lip, she grabbed a cloth, wiping her hands as she dashed for the door. She opened it and smiled at Peter. "Hey."

"You wanted this?" He extended the newspaper.

"Yeah. Thanks." She clasped the cool paper tightly, not even glancing at the front page. "You didn't have to bring it over quite so early."

"I knew you'd be up painting."

"I was." She stepped back. "Want to come in? Have some coffee?"

"Nah. Dad's fixing breakfast." He leaned toward her, his voice low. "Are you going to be okay with Forest seeing this?"

"Is it bad?"

"Let's just say there's more than your accolades about him in it."

"Oh, no." She held up the front page to the light. "Reporter Makes Mistake" leaped out at her. Groan. "Alison wrote a retraction on the same day I wrote a—"

"What's going on?" Forest entered the living room holding a cup of coffee. "Morning, Peter."

"Forest." Peter met Paige's gaze. "Talk to you later?"

"Sure. Thanks for bringing this by."

"No problem."

Paige closed the door.

"Why did Peter bring you the paper at six a.m.?" Forest asked.

"I'm afraid I did something you might not like." She gulped, hating the feelings of guilt churning inside of her.

"Oh? What's that?" He dropped onto the couch, nursing his cup in his hands.

She sat down beside him, nervously thumbing through the pages of the small paper until she found the letters-to-the-editor section. The title, "Wife Sticks Up for Husband," twisted tension through her. Nothing to be done about Alison's fingerprints on her writing now. She folded the paper in half and passed it to Forest.

"You might as well see this. I'm sorry if it causes you any trouble. I meant it for good."

He stared at her for several seconds before his gaze turned toward the paper. His eyes widened. His jaw slackened. "Paige. What—"

"I had to do it." She sounded defensive even to her own ears.

"No, you—"

"Alison wrote some bad things about you, and I don't like it!" She met his gaze intensely. "Please, don't be mad at me. I did what I thought I should do."

She hadn't checked to see if Alison even published the letter the way she wrote it.

Forest sighed, then read out loud, "'He's the most honorable man I've ever met. Anyone who read the editor's description of him and believed her words has been misled. I challenge you to embrace Forest as a kind and helpful member of our community.'" He closed his eyes for a moment, then met her gaze again. "You shouldn't have done this."

"I didn't want Alison, or Mia, getting the last say. I want people in my hometown to like you and appreciate you." She linked her hand around the crook of his elbow. "Please, understand. You're a part of this town now, and my family. I needed to stand up for you."

"Ahh, baby." He set down his cup and the newspaper on the coffee table. "Come here."

He opened his arms, and she fell against his chest, so grateful when he wrapped both his arms around her, holding her close against him, smoothing his hand down the back of her hair. Their sighs coincided. Thankfully, he wasn't angry with her. Or if he was, he hid his reaction well.

"'He's an honest man who holds my heart,'" Forest quoted her words near her ear. "Is that how you feel about me?"

"I meant every word." She pushed back enough to meet his gaze. "Are you upset with me?"

"Yes," he said without hesitation. "It's an open case I cannot comment on. One you shouldn't have commented on, either."

She nodded but didn't say anything.

"You're a state's witness too." He let go of his hold on her. "Whether you like it or not, you are involved in Edward Grant's trial."

"I know." She hated the idea of testifying in January, but she'd do her part to get justice for Paisley.

He stroked a strand of hair back from her cheek. "Why now?"

"What do you mean?"

"Why write this before Christmas? It's been four weeks since the other article. The gossip's dying down." He shrugged. "Won't this stir up talk again? I thought you hated that."

"I do. I just couldn't let go of what Alison said about you." She scooted slightly away from him. "Others in town wrote letters to her too."

His eyes widened. "Were you behind those?"

"Yes. Aunt Callie and I."

"Oh, man."

"Alison asked for my letter, so I—"

"Wait. What?"

"Yesterday she came into the gallery and—" Paige pictured the headline. "I mentioned the letter I might write, and she acted so enthusiastic." She picked up the newspaper and flipped to the front page. "Look at this. Maybe I fell for a trick."

They both clutched the paper from opposite sides and read Alison's article, letting out simultaneous moans. A. Riley wrote she "may have leaped to judgment against the local detective, but the jury was still out on her decision about his character."

"Is this a retraction or another dig at an open wound?" Forest asked.

"The headline seems like an apology. The article? Not so much." Paige leaned against the back of the couch. "Forest, I'm sorry. I honestly wanted to make things better. Not worse."

He tossed the paper on the coffee table, put his arm over her shoulder, and tugged her closer to his side. "It'll be okay. We'll figure this out."

She hoped so.

Now Alison might be coming to dinner with Craig? Paige didn't even want to break that news to Forest.

Thirty-nine

After Paige and Piper left, Forest spent the morning digging up the footings for the swing set in the backyard. He needed a distraction and a way to expend some energy. The whole damaged contraption had to go. Judah was coming over to lend a hand too. With two days until Christmas Eve, Forest was cutting it close. But the new swing set he'd ordered would be arriving tomorrow.

While he worked, his thoughts churned about the article Alison wrote, and about Paige's piece too. His wife meant well. But why was Alison causing him so much trouble?

"Hey." Judah, wearing work gloves and a navy knit hat, strode around the corner.

"Morning." Forest nodded toward him.

"Piper's going to love the new playset."

"Yeah, she will," Forest said without much enthusiasm.

"What do you want me to do?"

"Take the metal pieces apart." Forest thrust his shovel into the earth. "I'm digging up the old cement."

"Will do."

The men worked in silence for twenty minutes. The hard labor was satisfying after Forest's frustration over yet another newspaper debacle. What he wouldn't give for a few minutes to question Alison about her animosity toward him. Too bad Sheriff Morris wouldn't approve of such a conversation.

He groaned for what felt like the fiftieth time this morning.

"Care to tell me what's going on?" Judah held up the electric drill he was using to unscrew bolts. "You've been heaving sighs ever since I got here. Did something happen between you and Paige?"

Forest wiped the sweat from his brow. "You haven't read this morning's paper?"

"Nope." He tightened the nose on the drill. "What's in the paper?"

"Another article about me. Paige wrote something I wish she hadn't, too."

"So you're stewing on it?" Judah buzzed the drill in the air a couple of times.

"Stewing. Fighting the temptation to march into the newspaper office and give A. Riley a piece of my mind."

Judah chuckled. "Fighting it, huh?"

"Yeah." Forest held up his shovel. "Working off my firebrand angst the best I can."

"Been there, done that." Judah pointed upward. "What's God's will in this? Have you thought to ask?"

Forest felt a kick in the gut. Ask God what His will might be about him getting lambasted in the local paper?

"No, I didn't pray about it. The whole thing seems more like the enemy's plot than anything spiritually edifying."

"I beg to differ. His ways are mysterious."

"So I've heard. What am I supposed to glean from this experience?" The chip on his shoulder seemed to grow bigger by the second. "That I have too much pride? I should let whoever say whatever they want about me and not be bothered by it?"

"Hey, I'm not the enemy here."

"No, you're not." Forest slammed his shovel into the ground and dug deeper than before. He let the point of the shovel strike the cement a couple of times, glad for the jarring motion shaking through him. Yeah, he was mad. But why take his anger out on his brother-in-law? "Sorry. I'm not in the best humor."

"No problem." Judah returned to removing screws and bolts from the swing set. After a few minutes, he paused. "Have you heard Alison might be Craig's plus-one for Christmas Eve?"

"You've got to be kidding me."

"Paisley saw them together in Bert's." Judah shrugged. "If that happens, I hope you can swallow your pride, and set aside this newspaper business to be hospitable to her and Craig."

Forest groaned. "I appreciate what Craig did in divulging information about Evie. Because of that, Paige is safe. So is Paisley. But sharing dinner with him and Alison? After the two articles she wrote about me? Chatting with her like a hot coal isn't burning in my gut?" Forest clenched his jaw. "Not sure if I can."

"Trust me. You can."

"You're so certain because—?"

"Let's see." Judah glanced toward the darkening sky as if pondering the coming rain. "Something along the lines of … 'the one who is in you is greater than the one who is in the world.' Something about God's grace being greater than any frustrations within us."

A balloon-deflating sigh seeped out of Forest. He couldn't argue the scripture or Judah's view about grace. He'd need more strength than he had right now to sit across the table from Alison on Christmas Eve and not say something rude.

Judah took down the metal top piece from the swing set. "Something to pray about?"

"Yep." Forest kept digging but tension and pride gnawed at him.

"God's grace gets us through a lot of stuff." Judah adjusted his gloves. "Don't you think it'll be hard having Craig at the family table for the first time, him at the same table with my mother? And my wife? Every time he looks at her, I might want to deck him."

"I hadn't thought about that." Forest wiped the sweat off his forehead with the back of his forearm. "He and Paige were involved for a while too, as you know."

"Yeah. But Paisley and I were married. She and I are praying about it. Trusting God to help us to be kind and gracious." Judah shrugged a couple of times. "Craig might not show up. He told me no. But I have a hunch he'll show up just to spite me." He chuckled. "In truth, I'll be glad if he does. We'll get through the other stuff."

They worked in silence for several minutes.

"One other thing. Be praying for Peter and Ruby, will you?"

"What's going on?"

"Just pray. You and I understand how challenging reconciliation can be." Judah stuffed some screws and bolts into his jacket. "They could use our prayer support right now."

"Will do."

For the next while, Forest tried letting go of his negative feelings toward Alison so he could focus on praying for his brother-and-sister-in-law. Then he added a prayer for Teal and Danson and their two boys. It seemed he had a lot of family stuff to be praying about.

Forty

Ruby breathed deeply of the sea air, enjoying the familiar scents she'd grown accustomed to during her years as a laborer on a fishing boat. Beside her, Sarah picked up shells and pretty rocks, seemingly enjoying their beach walk.

"This is lovely," Sarah said, tipping her face up to the sunshine. "I haven't felt this alive in such a long while."

"That's great. Do you want to keep walking?"

"Yes, please."

They hiked slowly across the mudflats, each of them commenting on some of nature's treasures—a stone with fool's gold in it, an interesting piece of driftwood, a unique shell.

"May I ask you something?" Sarah fingered a rock.

"Sure."

"Why aren't you and Peter together?"

Ruby froze, momentarily shocked by the personal question.

"Sorry." Sarah dropped the stone. "If it's too private of a topic, that's okay."

Ruby didn't care to discuss Peter's and her relationship with anyone. But she didn't want to shut the door on conversing with Sarah, either. Maybe if she told a small part of her story, perhaps Sarah would open up a little more, too.

Walking parallel to the tideline, Ruby reminisced about her and Peter living on a fishing boat, about some funny mishaps involving fish, and skirted personal issues.

Sarah gave her a long look. "You have shared experiences with him. And friendship?"

"Yes."

"But you're not together. Something must have happened." Sarah stared out toward the incoming waves. "Was he mean? Unfaithful?"

"Goodness, no. We just grew apart."

Out in the bay, an orca leaped out of the water, almost clearing the waves before diving under again.

"Did you see that?" Sarah asked excitedly.

"Yeah. That was awesome."

While she and Sarah watched for the killer whale to break the surface of the water again, Ruby told her about a pod of orcas she and Peter had seen in Alaskan waters. How they leaped in and out of the water around the perimeter of the *Lily Forever* as if they were playing a game of Ring Around the Rosie.

Sarah chuckled. Then, seemingly out of the blue, said, "I was married."

"You were?"

Her shoulders sagged like her emotional burden was too heavy to carry. "It's difficult for me to talk about. But these people"—she nodded back the way they'd come—"and you have helped me breathe normally again."

"I'm glad you're feeling better."

"I get why you don't want to talk about your marriage." Sarah shrugged and walked back toward the project house.

Ruby quickly caught up with her.

"But my future"—Sarah took a breath—"isn't as lost as I thought it was before. Even seeing those pictures of my granny when she was a girl was sweet and nostalgic. Healing, even."

Ruby was surprised by her sudden openness.

"Thank you for helping me find hope." Sarah stopped walking and clasped Ruby's hand.

"I didn't do anything."

"You were here." She gave Ruby's hand a squeeze, then released it. "Someone I could tell was struggling too."

They walked again, and Ruby kept stride with Sarah. "Peter and I have our hurdles to cross. But being here is helping me too."

"I wish I still had the chance to work things out with my husband," Sarah said in a far-off voice.

Why couldn't she work things out with him? Were they divorced? Had he married someone else?

"He died last year."

"I'm so sorry." Ruby hugged her. "What happened?"

"A car accident on Christmas Eve." Sarah stepped back from the hug. "When Jeremy died, I thought I'd die too. Even hearing Christmas songs this year was unbearable. I took off, not caring where I ended up, or if I died along the way."

"Oh, Sarah."

"I don't feel so morbid, now."

"And you ended up at your grandmother's house." Ruby linked her arm with Sarah's. "That's kind of amazing."

"It is. But I miss him so much. How can I keep living when he didn't get a chance to do that?"

"I'm sorry for your loss. For your heartache."

"I'll always be grateful to Kathleen and the others for letting me stay with them. For caring." She looked Ruby in the eye. "If there was anything I could do, anything at all, to not have had that last argument with him, I would."

A weight pressed down on Ruby's heart as she heard herself telling Peter to stay away. If something terrible happened to him, wouldn't she feel awful if that was the last thing between them?

Forty-one

If one more person entered the newspaper office spouting rude comments, Ali might scream. First, Maggie Thomas came by. "You can shove your disgusting paper in the toilet for all I care!" The hardware store owner, Miss Patty, was next. "Stop causing strife. Leave us alone!"

Others called and left messages—"Leave town!" "Do yourself a favor and find another profession." "Take a long hike off a short bridge."

The door jangled, and Ali clenched her teeth.

Callie marched straight toward her, holding out a copy of the *Gazette*. "What's this about?" The woman plopped into the chair across from Ali. "Did you forget our agreement?"

"I acknowledged I may have made a mistake. Are you here to do your part?"

"Try again." Callie hurled the paper onto the cluttered desk. "This is not an apology. Not a retraction, either. It's more troublemaking. Write it again!"

"I will not." Ali jumped to her feet. "I'm sick and tired of this town's small-mindedness. If you're here to harass me into writing what you want, just … just leave."

She couldn't take any more insults. Why did Uncle Milton leave her the task of finding out the truth in Basalt Bay when he wasn't willing to stick around and search it out himself?

"Well, then, maybe we're finally getting somewhere," Callie said smugly.

"What?"

Callie nodded toward Ali's chair, one eyebrow quirked.

Groaning, she dropped onto the edge of her seat.

"I got a text from Paige saying you and that snake in the grass might be coming to our Christmas Eve family dinner."

"What of it?"

Callie grabbed the paper again. "With this begrudging attitude you have toward my niece's husband, are doubts and suspicions what you'll be bringing to our holiday meal?"

"Is your precious dinner what this discussion is about?" Ali let the irritation she felt swell into her voice. "I doubt I'll step foot in your house. Why would I put myself through that?"

"Why, indeed?" Callie squinted at her. "I don't mean to sound rude—"

Sure she didn't. Ali clenched her lips together.

"But you agreed to make an apology."

"I did not!"

"If you did, which you didn't, and against my better judgment, I agreed to tell you about our town." Callie's chest puffed up. "If you won't make an honest retraction—"

"You know where the door is." Ali jumped up again.

"I certainly do." With some effort, Callie pushed out of her chair and shuffled to the exit. "Why did Milton leave the way he did?"

"I don't know."

"He left and dropped the business in your lap? Doesn't that sound suspicious?"

"Yes, it does." Tears filled Ali's eyes, but she blinked fast. She would not cry in front of Callie Cedars.

The thought of Uncle Milton possibly sweeping Mayor Grant's wrongs under the rug like a servant doing his master's dirty deeds cut her to the quick. She silently begged Callie to leave, because she certainly didn't plan to talk about it.

"I'm sorry for my comment about you joining our holiday dinner." Callie's face hued rosy. "I don't want you to avoid us because of something you wrote."

"No?" Isn't that exactly why she should avoid the Cedars/Grant hoopla?

"Seeing our family's flaws and how we've overcome past problems for the sake of Christmas and togetherness, you might realize you're wrong about some of your assumptions." Callie bobbed her chin and closed the door softly.

"Or I might find out I was right all along," Ali muttered.

Forty-two

Peter spent most of yesterday and today in his room, his emotions hitting the proverbial brick wall. Six days had passed since Ruby gave him that ultimatum. Three days since he talked with Judah. What did he say about grace? Something about it being a life-changer for him.

All this downtime was frustrating. Maybe Dad had some chores he could do. A room in need of painting. The attic cleaned. Anything to get rid of his angst.

Would prayer help like Judah said it would? As a kid, Peter listened to Pastor Sagle preach. Sunday school teachers taught him Bible stories. But had he ever embraced faith for himself? He did what he saw others do. Went to church. Read his Bible. But taking it all in for himself? Having faith when the chips were down? Probably not.

Judah's words skimmed through his thoughts. *"If we have grace for everyone, including for ourselves, what past sin or flaw can we hold over anyone?"*

"If" being the pivotal point.

As Peter sat on his old twin bed, he pondered some of the people in his life whom he'd held grievances against. Mom and Dad. Workers on his uncle's boat. Uncle Henry. He'd made plenty of mistakes too. Things he regretted.

Groaning, he leaned his back against the headboard and stole a few glances at the book on the nightstand. As a youth, he carried the green Bible with its ratty edges to church and Sunday school. The book had been part of his life, even if he hadn't fully embraced the faith message, before he left Basalt Bay in a rage. Talk about offenses. He hadn't read a Bible in twelve years, either. Too stubborn. Determined to do things his own way.

He smoothed his rough finger pads over the cover of the old book. When did he stop believing in God? Maybe during the arguments he had with Mom and Dad. Or when he felt so much wretched need to get away from Basalt Bay.

That was the thing with small towns. Kids either grew up loving that lifestyle and wanting to raise their own families in the small-town environment, or else they hated it and wanted out! He'd been a part of the latter group. Somewhere along the way, his heart hardened toward his parents and toward God.

He picked up the Bible, fingering where the gold lettering had faded away. What would it hurt to read a few verses? Maybe then he'd feel like praying. Was God even interested in his life? In his marriage? In how poorly the relationship between him and Ruby had been lately? He thumbed through the pages. Familiar names—Matthew, Mark, Luke, John— leaped out at him.

He settled on John, since he recalled enjoying that book as a teenager. Twenty-one chapters later, he sighed and closed the Bible. He pressed his fingertips against his forehead.

That last fishing story, the one in chapter twenty-one, had especially caught his interest. He related to the disciples fishing all night and not catching a single thing. The disappointment. Financial failure. Public embarrassment. Wrecked pride. The whole thing reminded him of himself on some of his fishing expeditions.

Then Jesus stood on the shore, and his friends didn't even recognize Him? What kind of friends were they? He told them to try fishing again.

After fishing all night and not catching anything, would Peter follow anyone's advice to try again? He was stubborn and determined to do things his way. Maybe those were things he and Jesus's disciple, Peter, in the Bible had in common.

Overcoming discouragement and self-doubt, the disciples did what Jesus said and caught an abundance of fish! Of course, then they realized who the man on the shore was who told them to go fishing again. Peter leaped into the water— how impulsive was that?—swimming for Jesus with all his might. A new beginning. Full of faith. He was all in, then. Doubts gone.

Peter sighed. Oh, to experience a faith like that! Such a lack of doubt.

A powerful wave of emotion, maybe of spiritual longing, hit him. The Peter in the story wasn't the only one needing a new beginning. Peter craved a fresh start, too. Not just with Ruby. Not just with Dad. But with God. Within himself.

Jesus. Lord. Help.

Not an eloquent prayer, but heartfelt. He longed for relief from the inner battle. He wanted peace.

He thumbed through the New Testament again, reading verses he'd underlined years ago. Several caught his attention. He read one verse in Colossians three times. "'... he has reconciled you by Christ's physical body through death to present you holy in his sight, without blemish and free from accusation—if you continue in your faith ...'"

"He has reconciled you," repeated in his thoughts. Did he want to be reconciled to God? Free from accusation? Without blemish? Continuing in faith?

Judah said grace was about not holding things over others. Not even holding things over himself.

Could Peter let go of the past? His pride? The hurtful memories? The things he wished he could undo? The things he held onto as if they were a part of his very soul?

Ever since I left, I've held a grudge. Can You heal me, God? Change me so I can be more like You? In myself, I don't think it's possible.

He imagined Pastor Sagle long ago saying, "Trust God. With Him everything is possible."

Was that just a platitude some people spouted like magical words of wisdom? Did Pastor Sagle truly believe the words? Did he still, even after all these years?

Was everything possible if Peter believed? If so, could he hold onto that belief in the future? Even when things got rough?

An hour later, after poring over more verses and praying, he jogged down the stairs with a powerful feeling of hope and fresh belief, maybe trust in God's hand in his life, running through him. There was a matter he had to see to immediately. A relationship to repair, if possible.

"Dad?" he said as soon as he stepped into the living room. "Can we talk?"

"Sure." Dad fumbled for the TV remote, shutting off the noise in the room.

Peter dropped onto the couch, settling his elbows against his thighs. He'd thought this through, but his upper torso trembled at what he was about to say. "I, well, I, uh, need to say something to you."

"All right."

"I'm sorry for how I left you and Mom all those years ago." He gulped. "I was angry. Resentful. I left in a stupid rage. That was wrong. I wish I could undo that."

Dad's eyes filled with moisture. "What brought this on?"

"I just—" Peter cleared his throat. "I decided to pray. Trust in Jesus. I'm sorry for how I treated you and Mom. I left without talking things through. I was disrespectful and arrogant." Hard to admit, yet the tenderness of knowing Christ, feeling pure again, made him humbler than he had ever been. Saying this now was the right thing to do. "I'm sorry for holding a grudge against you for all these years, too."

"Oh, Son. I'm the one who's sorry. Your mom and I made mistakes." Dad sniffed. "I'm sorry our choices caused you to leave too soon."

Both men stood. Dad reached out his hand as if to shake Peter's. But Peter wrapped his arms around his father's shoulders. "I love you, Dad."

"Love you too, Son." They patted each other's backs.

Then they chuckled.

Wiping his eyes, Dad said, "Us hugging and crying? Who'd believe it?"

"God would." Peter sniffed and cleared his throat. "It's kind of awesome."

Dad sagged into his chair. "Are you going to talk to Ruby now?"

Peter dropped back onto the couch cushion. "I hope so. She and I have a lot to work out. I love her. Don't want to lose her."

"You won't because you're going to do everything within your power to make things right and win her back, aren't you?"

This time he didn't resent his father's advice.

"With God's help, I will." An awareness of the Lord in his life poured through Peter's core like a cool stream over dry rocks. "I can't wait to tell her what's happened. She won't believe it."

Dad chuckled. "This might be exactly what she's been waiting for. Praying about, even."

"You think so?"

"Talk to her. See for yourself." A wobbly smile spread across Dad's lips.

Would his heartfelt apology be the proof of his love Ruby was looking for?

Forty-three

Paisley joined the ladies at the project house as they worked together, baking desserts, dinner rolls, and prepping finger foods for the Christmas Eve celebration tomorrow. Bess was mixing brownies. Aunt Callie worked on pie fillings. Kathleen and Sarah were rolling out sugar cookie dough. And Paisley was chopping veggies.

While Sarah seemed quiet whenever Paisley was around, Aunt Callie said their visitor confided in Ruby about being a widow in search of a new start. Having needed a fresh start herself, Paisley was thankful Sarah had discovered some stability here among these kind ladies.

Tears flooded her eyes. She sure was emotional lately.

Kathleen and Sarah chuckled over something, looking almost like grandmother and granddaughter.

"Did you ever make cookies like these when you were growing up?" Kathleen asked.

"Yes. When I was little."

The chatter in the room grew quiet, making hearing Sarah's soft voice easier.

"My brother and I made sugar cookies with our mom." Sarah patted some dough with her hand. "We used to fight over who got to make the star-shaped cookies. They were our favorite because we sprinkled yellow-tinted sugar on top."

Kathleen dug into a canister on the butcher-block island. "I have just the thing." She pulled out a star cookie cutter and passed it to Sarah. "Try this."

Sarah lifted the metal shape and held it gingerly as if it was a prized treasure. "Thank you, Kathleen."

A wad of emotion thickened in Paisley's throat.

"Make all the sugar cookie stars you'd like, dear." Kathleen sidearm hugged her.

"Thank you. You've been so kind to me." Sarah glanced around, including the rest of them. "Thank you all."

"You're welcome." Kathleen blinked quickly. "Now, let's get some more of these made. The children will be arriving tomorrow. They're going to love star cookies with yellow sugar sprinkled on top."

Sarah grinned and nodded.

"They aren't the only ones," Aunt Callie muttered.

"That's right." Paisley imagined biting into a sugar cookie and drinking holiday tea. Maybe someday she'd be making cute cookies with her own daughter.

The room broke into chatter again, happy sounds of laughter and banter over childhood memories and cookie recipes filling the room. Warm feelings of family and closeness enveloped Paisley. So did thoughts of her possible Christmas Eve announcement. Tomorrow morning she'd take the pregnancy test. If it was positive, she'd tell Judah at the gazebo after Paige and Forest's vow renewal. What a memorable night it was going to be!

Wouldn't he be thrilled? He'd probably get teary-eyed, his deep blue irises shimmering. Then he'd kiss her—a sweet, meaningful kiss full of love and devotion. Such tender emotions came over her. Oh, she loved him and their life together.

She adored imagining the family they would have. How many children? Two? Three? She'd always think of Misty Gale as her firstborn. Maybe this one, if there was a child inside her, would be a boy who looked like Judah.

She fought the impulse to stroke her hand over her tummy. She didn't want to bring attention to herself with such a move and what it might mean. Tomorrow was soon enough.

She liked the idea of having a child soon so Piper and this baby could grow up together. Maybe the two of them would run on the beach like Paisley and Peter had done when they were kids. Maybe not quite as daring and mischievous as she and Peter were. But the seashore being their playground? She wished that for her child with her whole heart.

"What has your thoughts captivated?" Bess peered at Paisley. "Your face is nearly glowing."

"Is it? Just daydreaming."

"About anything in particular?" Bess dropped little globs of peanut butter over the brownie mixture.

"Oh, um, well—"

"I'm sorry. You have a right to keep your thoughts private."

Paisley knew her mother-in-law didn't mean to pry. She appreciated her even caring about her thoughts. She'd like to tell her she might be a grandmother, but Judah should be the first to hear. Still, she leaned her shoulder against Bess's.

"Just imagining those somedays in the future."

"Anything in particular?"

"Children. A bigger house. Don't get me wrong. I love our beach cabin."

"I know you do. You are so good for my son, sweet daughter-in-love." Bess hugged her.

Paisley smiled at the endearment. "Thanks. I'm content with my life."

"And looking forward to a bright future?"

"A very bright future."

Glancing over her shoulder, she met Sarah's gaze. Had she been listening? Hard not to do in this intimate setting of five ladies baking together. Paisley smiled at her new friend, wishing for a brighter future for her too.

Forty-four

That afternoon, Peter stepped into the entryway of the project house, eager to speak with his wife. "Is Ruby here?"

Aunt Callie crossed her arms like a guard, her body blocking him from moving forward. His own aunt wasn't going to let him enter the house where Ruby was staying?

"Last I heard, she wanted space away from you. What's that about, Nephew?"

The heat of irritation filling Peter's brain conflicted with his new desire to live in peace and grace. "Aunt Callie, I love you, but Ruby and I have to work this out by ourselves. Do you want to call her? Or should I bellow for her myself?"

He stared at her for about thirty seconds, a warfare of gazes ricocheting between them.

"Ruby!" she finally yelled. "Your impatient husband is here to see you!"

"Thank you." He took a step back and clasped his hands together, trying not to look so intense.

"Ruby!" Aunt Callie called again, not moving from her bulldog stance.

Finally, when Ruby strolled down the stairs, Aunt Callie gave Peter a warning look before shuffling into the kitchen.

"Hey, Rube." He smiled at her.

She looked so beautiful in her golden sweater with her long red hair hanging over her shoulders. He'd missed seeing her. He wanted to embrace her and tell her everything on his heart.

"I thought I told you—"

"I need to talk with you. Please?"

"Has anything changed?" She eyed him.

"Yes. Something has changed. May I explain? Can we talk privately?"

She stared at him for a few moments. "Okay."

"I've missed you, Rube."

She didn't smile at him. Didn't give him any hope of wanting to reconcile with him. She glanced toward the door. "We can talk outside. Maybe on the porch?"

"Sure. That works for me." He swayed his hand for her to precede him.

Aunt Callie pegged him with another look from the kitchen before he went outside and closed the door.

A misty rain fell beyond the covered porch. Ruby crossed her arms and kept a couple of feet between them. "What did you want to talk about?"

"You. Me. And forever?" All the things he wanted to tell her burned in his chest like a fire about to combust. But most of all, he wanted to assure her of his love. "I love you, Rube."

She squinted at him. "And—?"

"Will you sit with me?" He nodded toward the porch steps that didn't look too damp.

"Okay." She sat down stiffly, keeping space between them. She seemed reluctant to even be here with him. Would she listen to him? Give him another chance?

Lord, please help me with this.

* * * *

Why was Peter here? He said something had changed. But what?

"Why are you smiling at me?" She crossed her arms.

He had the audacity to laugh!

"Peter!" She started to stand up. If he wasn't going to be serious—

"Ruby, hold up. Sorry." He clasped her arm briefly, then let go. "Please, stay. I really do want us to talk. I have so much to share with you."

She lowered herself back to the step.

"I meant what I said. I have missed you." He drew in a full breath like he needed the air for strength. "I miss us being back in our boat too. But the truth is you're what matters to me." He clasped her hand and smoothed his fingers over hers. "Wherever you are, that's where I want to be. And I'm not saying any of this just to tell you what I think you want me to say."

She met his gaze and read sincerity in his moist eyes.

"I don't want to keep staying with my dad if you aren't staying there with me."

"You don't get to decide that for me." She pulled her hand away, clasping her own hands in her lap.

"No, but I'm telling you what's on my heart. I'm being completely honest." He tilted his head, staring at her deeply. "I want us to be married again. You and me loving each other, being there for each other, looking out for one another the way we did in our first year of marriage."

His tender words stirred up longings within her. Wasn't him being able to express his feelings what she'd been waiting for? Hoping for? The way he was being open and sharing his thoughts, now, was a change. So was his saying she was what mattered to him.

"I love you more than anyone or anything in this whole world."

A breath caught in her throat. Moisture flooded her eyes.

He set his palms gently on her shoulders. Their gazes tangled. Moisture filled his eyes too. "I'm so sorry for hurting you. For erecting walls. For turning inward and becoming a grumpy curmudgeon." He smiled at her as if he was looking right into her heart.

Oh, Peter.

"You were right to be offended at the careless way I treated you. How I demanded my own way about the boat, not having kids, and not buying a house."

He took a long breath, which gave her the chance to breathe too. Where was he going with all this?

Removing his hands from her shoulders, he linked her fingers loosely with his. "I've been praying about our situation and us."

"You have?" Nothing he could have said would have shocked her as much as him saying he'd been praying for them. "You've been praying about us?"

"I have." He grinned. "I talked with Judah. Read the book of John in the Bible. I talked to God. I even apologized to my dad."

"Really?" This ... Peter admitting his faults and even talking to his dad was a huge change from his previous actions.

Peter nodded. "Here I am, apologizing to you, the woman I love more than any other person on the planet. The woman I want to be with for the rest of my life." He squeezed her hands lightly as if confirming his points. "I know I've messed up in more ways than I care to admit. But will you forgive me? Can we start over? You and me forever like we said in the beginning?"

He gave her the sweetest smile, and her heart melted into a mushy puddle of love and acceptance. Forgiveness, too. He touched his lips softly against hers. Leaning back, he met her gaze as if asking if kissing her was okay.

She nodded slightly. A sob came close to bursting out of her, but she held it back. She wasn't going to get all sappy. She wanted to pay attention to everything he was saying.

"You told me to prove my love to you. I thought, how in the world can I do that?" Another smile crossed those lips that were recently pressed against hers. "I could buy you a diamond ring. But my Ruby doesn't like diamonds."

She chuckled.

"I could buy you a new car. Would buying a vehicle prove my love to you?"

She shook her head, going along with his teasing.

"My wife wouldn't want jewelry or a car as a sign of her husband's love." A serious expression crossed his face. "I even thought of buying you a house."

"Peter, you didn't."

"Would that prove my love to you?"

"Not really." Although, it would have shown her he'd been listening to what she asked of him.

Extravagant purchases weren't the answer. But the way he was talking to her, his tender kisses, and how he said he prayed for them? These things meant a great deal to her. They were a leap toward healing the hurts in her heart.

Peter gazed into her eyes so tenderly and unreservedly. With each glimmer of his sparkling irises, her heart flip-flopped in her chest like a butterfly dancing against glass. Still clutching her hands, he dropped to his knee in front of her.

"Peter?"

"Rube, will you forgive me for being a killjoy? For the way I treated you like an employee more than a sweet wife whom I adored?" He blew out a breath like he was controlling his emotions too. "I'm sorry I did that. And just so you know, this apology comes without strings. I'm not saying this stuff to get you to come back to the *Lily Forever* with me. Although, I do want you back with me like I want my next breath. It isn't to get you to share your bed with me, either, but"—a teasing smile crossed his lips—"I want that too."

She couldn't help smiling back at him. "You don't have to be on your knee, Peter. The ground is wet."

"I'm staying right here until you say you forgive me." He kissed the back of her right hand, then her left. "Please? Will you let me love you again? Will you love me as your husband?"

Her thoughts fled back to Sarah saying she'd do anything for the last thing between her and her husband to have not been an argument.

"Do you mean it? The apology, the yearning for things to be right between us?"

"I do. You are the only woman for me. From here on out, the *Lily Forever* comes only after you in my devotion and love."

The air expelled from her lungs. For him to say she was more important than the *Lily Forever* was ginormous! Ruby's eyes flooded with tears, and she didn't fight them this time.

"Do you forgive me?"

"I do." She dropped to her knees in front of him, right on the wet gravel. Their gazes locked, she leaned into him and kissed him fully on the mouth. His warm lips caressed hers, his arms wrapping around her, holding her close to him.

"Thank you for coming back to me," she whispered.

"Thank you for giving us another chance."

Holding hands, they stood. Then they sat on the porch together, talking, kissing, and sharing their hearts some more. Soon, they were curled up in each other's arms again, their backs against the side of the project house, the rain falling all around them, their two hearts, finally, beating as one.

Forty-five

Paige closed the gallery early on Christmas Eve. As she drove home after picking up Piper from Dad's, she thought about Forest's and her discussion last night. He was so sweet when he said he didn't blame her for writing that letter to the editor, which was a huge relief. He also explained about the more recent threat concerning the art gala. An unnerving detail. But they talked it over, and to be on the safe side, she agreed to putting the event off indefinitely. The gallery was doing fine without a grand opening, anyway.

She apologized to him for her abrupt behavior when Piper spilled juice on her painting a week ago—something she should have mentioned before now. He seemed relieved by her apology. When she brought up Craig and Alison possibly coming to the family dinner, he acted tense. But with the articles Alison wrote, who could blame him?

Married only a month and a half, they had some kinks to work out in their relationship. But it felt good for them to be getting things out in the open and working on their marriage together.

Just as she took Piper out of her car seat, Forest jogged into the carport. "Hey, you two," he said, grinning.

Since he texted her earlier, she knew he was ready to show Piper the surprise he'd been working on.

"Hey, princess."

Piper giggled and thrust out her arms to him.

He scooped her up. "Daddy has a Christmas surprise you're going to love. Come on." He leaned in and kissed Paige's cheek. "Hey, baby. Welcome home."

"Thank you. I'm so glad to be here." Not wanting to miss a second of his gift reveal, she shut the car door and scurried after him and Piper.

Forest took long strides toward the shiny new red swing set in the backyard. "Merry Christmas, Piper!"

Paige glanced between Piper's smiling face and Forest's big grin. Both of their matching gazes were aimed at the swing set.

"Swing! Swing!"

"That's right. See what Daddy and Uncle Judah built for you?" Forest set her down.

Paige slid her phone out of her pocket and snapped a few candid shots of Piper running to the swing, and Forest following her.

"Merry Christmas, princess." He kissed Piper's cheek and set her on the black swing. "I hope this swing set gives you lots of fun and joy for years to come."

"Swing, swing," Piper chanted.

"Hold on tight."

Paige stepped back, taking it all in, watching Forest and Piper together on this first Christmas Eve, sharing in their happy moments.

Barring any other destructive hurricanes, this swing set should last through the next ten years or so. Through more children playing on it, too. She'd hoped to make an announcement to Forest this Christmas, but it wasn't to be. Maybe next month. She was so eager for them to add another member to their family.

Piper's laughter brought her back to the scene before her. Forest was pushing Piper gently. Piper held onto the chains and laughed with each forward motion as if the air tickled her face.

"Do you like it, Pipe?" Paige asked.

"*Yike* it!"

"You did good, Forest. What a great Christmas surprise."

"Thanks." His smile got even bigger.

"Shall we grab some lunch? I'm hungry." She nodded toward the house. "Are your folks in town yet?"

He pushed Piper again. "Yes, about lunch. According to Mom's text, they'll be arriving within the hour. They're going to head straight to the inn and unwind before dinner."

"I hope everything works out okay for them there."

"Me too." He brought the swing to a stop.

"Swing!" Piper called out.

Forest shrugged toward Paige. "Maybe a few more minutes, huh?"

"Try the slide. Getting her off the swing might help her adjust before going inside for lunch." She took a few steps toward the back porch. "I'll get sandwiches started. I need to throw a roast in the cooker for tonight's dinner, too. Won't take long."

"Sounds good." Forest squatted down next to Piper. "How about trying the slide?"

"*Swide?*"

"That's right. Then we'll go inside for some of Mommy's yummy lunch." He met Paige's gaze and winked at her. "Love you."

"Love you too," she said, appreciating the joys of marriage and co-parenting with this sweet man.

She hurried into the house, thinking of the Christmas present she'd be giving him tonight. They agreed not to buy each other presents. Instead, they were giving one another a meaningful gift. She'd thought and thought about what she could give him. It was their first Christmas together. She wanted to do something special for him.

Finally, recalling the way Forest gazed longingly at the photos on the mantle of Piper with other family members, she had the perfect idea. She couldn't wait to show him the gift she made for him!

Forty-six

"Mom! Dad!" Forest hugged his parents who just arrived at the project house.

"Good to see you." Dad looked festive with his grayish-black hair slicked back and wearing a snowman tie. He shook Forest's hand, and his grayish-green eyes, so much like Forest's and Piper's, gleamed.

"Where's our granddaughter?" Mom shuffled the wrapped packages in her arms and gave Forest a huge hug. "I can't wait to meet her."

"Paige took her for a walk down to the beach. She'll be back shortly. You want me to help with those?"

"I'll do that." Dad grabbed hold of some of Mom's load.

Forest introduced his folks to the ladies of the house who were all busy working in the kitchen. "These are my parents, Bob and Janey Harper."

"Welcome." Kathleen hugged both as if they were old friends.

"Merry Christmas Eve!" Bess called cheerily from where she stood by the oven stirring something in a pot.

"Glad you made it safely," Callie said.

"Thank you. What a lovely house you have," Mom said.

"We have Judah, Forest, Ruby, and a few others to thank for that." Bess grinned.

Thundering footsteps on the porch preceded his nephews, Tommy and Taylor. "Uncle Forest!" the two blonds chimed as they dodged through the doorway.

He met their exuberant hugs and roughed up their hair. "Good to see you guys. Where's your—"

"I'm right behind them." Flipping long platinum bangs out of her eyes, Teal strode through the doorway with a red tote overflowing with wrapped gifts. Exasperation blared from her face.

"Let me help, Sis." He hugged her and took hold of the tote. "How are you?"

She nodded toward the boys. "Traveling with two rambunctious four-year-olds has its moments."

"I bet." Chuckling, Forest strode toward the bigger room. "Come in here and see the tree."

"A tree. Oh, boy," Tommy said.

"Beat you," Taylor trilled.

The boys raced around Forest and charged into the living room.

"Tommy! Taylor!" Their grandpa called from the other room.

"Hold up, you two!" Teal's grimace said it all. She was exhausted, and her vacation had just started.

215

Forest texted Paige that his family arrived. A few minutes later, she and Piper joined them.

Paige and Mom hugged. They met in Portland a couple of weeks ago when Forest closed his apartment and got his car. During that visit, they all went out to lunch, but he and Paige didn't bring Piper along. Instead, they used it as a getaway for themselves, since they hadn't had a real honeymoon.

Mom oohed and aahed over Piper. Piper warmed right up to her grandma. Tommy and Taylor gave their cousin stiff hugs at Teal's prompting. Then they ran off to play in the woods with warnings from their mom to stay close and to not go near the water.

Forest almost objected. Would his feisty nephews stay close to the house just because their mother said so? If they were anything like he was as a kid, and he knew they were, they'd be down at the seaside in two minutes. He'd check on them and help Teal out as much as he could while she was here.

Forest settled his arm over Paige's shoulder. "You doing okay?"

"A little frazzled with all the gallery stuff and then getting the food ready. But, yeah, I'm okay."

He kissed her cheek. "Think you can relax now?"

"Hope so."

"Me too. It's going to be a lovely evening."

She met his gaze with a questioning look.

"Oh, uh, it's our first Christmas together," he said quickly, hoping he hadn't given anything away.

"I know. I'm so thankful for that. For you." She kissed his cheek.

"Maybe you'll have a surprise for me later?" he asked playfully.

"Maybe."

"Good." Hopefully, no one would say anything about the vow renewal, so he could pull off his surprise for her.

Soon, everyone was assigned tasks in preparation for the Christmas Eve meal. Callie barked orders like a drill sergeant. The delicious scents of food cooking filled the room, making his mouth water. The ladies bustled around setting out plates and yummy-looking dishes.

"Shall I check on the boys?" Forest asked Teal.

"That would be great. Thanks, Bub."

He chuckled at her childhood nickname for him.

His thoughts turned toward the upcoming meal. Would Craig and Alison be joining them? He still felt a knot in his gut every time he thought of what she said about him in the paper. But he was trying to let the negative feelings go. Praying he could do so.

Forty-seven

At the Christmas Eve dinner, including two tables of fifteen adults, three kids, and two empty chairs, Ruby sat between Paisley and Peter, near Callie's end of the main table. Feeling her hand clasped with her husband's beneath the table, the rough pads of his fingers stroking her palm, she felt warmth course through her. Things were changing between them. Good changes. Peter's touch, his closeness, and even the spicy masculine scent of his deodorant and soap reminded her of their time spent on the porch yesterday. Of their kisses and cuddling too.

She met his gaze. He watched her closely, his eyes shining as if he had kissing on the brain also. Her cheeks heated up at the thought of them making their excuses and heading out to the porch later.

He grinned like he knew what she was thinking.

Callie cleared her throat. "Before Pauly says grace, I want to welcome all of you to the project house for our first Christmas Eve meal together." She eyed someone at the far side of the table, probably James. "May there be many more celebrations enjoyed here in the future."

Cheers went up around the table. The kids at the other table, sitting with Paige, Forest, and his parents and sister, clapped.

Footsteps thudded across the porch. Paige leaped up and ran for the door, even before the knock came.

"Craig! Alison. Welcome. Merry Christmas!"

"Sorry we're late," Craig said.

So this was Judah's half-brother? Ruby watched the man's dark gaze sweep across the group. His blond date— Ruby knew about Alison only from Callie's mutterings about her newspaper articles—stood beside him, furtively glancing around the room. No one was gabbing or laughing now. Tension crisscrossed the room alongside the exchange of glances.

Judah stood and shook Craig's hand. "Welcome."

"Thanks."

"Welcome, you guys," Paisley said from her seat. "Merry Christmas!"

Craig nodded at Paisley but didn't take a step toward the table.

"Food's getting cold," Callie said brusquely.

Ruby squeezed Peter's hand, feeling a little confused. Here was Judah, inviting an estranged family member to the table. Yet tension zinged around the room like two rocks hitting each other, sending off sparks.

Piper shoved away from her booster seat and ran toward her mom. Or maybe Craig.

"*Cag! Cag!*"

"Hey, Pipe." A smile crossed his face as he bent over and picked up Piper. "How's it going, kiddo?"

Piper patted his cheeks with both hands and laughed.

Paige smiled. "She's missed you."

"Yeah, me too. Merry Christmas, Pipe."

Piper said something cute and indistinguishable.

Ruby glanced over at Forest. What did he think of this newcomer interacting with Paige and Piper in such a friendly, almost intimate, manner? He thrust his hands through his hair as if he was dealing with stress or frustration. Ruby's attention went back to Craig and Paige.

"What a charmer you have," Alison said and patted Piper's back. "She's a cutie."

"Thank you." Paige scooped up Piper and took her back to her seat at the smaller table. As she sat down, she clasped Forest's hand. The two of them exchanged glances.

At once, the mutually held breath seemed to release.

"May I take your coats?" Judah asked.

"Sure." Craig removed his jacket and helped Alison with hers.

Callie let out a longsuffering groan and tapped a tense rhythm on the table with her fingernails.

Paul cleared his throat and glared at her. Callie glared right back at him.

But then, something interesting happened. Ruby probably wouldn't have noticed, except Callie had previously mentioned her secret fondness for James ever since she was a girl. Callie gave him a slight welcoming smile. James nodded once in her direction, almost imperceptibly. But Ruby saw it and hid a grin.

One of these days those two were going to explode with the need to tell each other how they felt. If peace and goodwill were possible, she prayed it would happen between Callie and James.

Judah showed Craig and Alison to their seats next to Paul, which were across from Judah and Paisley at the other side of the table.

"Now, can we pray and get on with our meal?" Callie asked in a perturbed tone. "The food's getting cold!"

Peter winked at Ruby on the sly. Then he rocked his eyebrows like he was conveying a flirty message to her.

On impulse, she kissed his rough cheek. "Merry Christmas, Peter."

His eyes pulsed wide. Was he surprised she'd do that with his family watching?

Peace and goodwill had to begin somewhere. Why not let it begin with them?

Forty-eight

When Paul told everyone to clasp hands before he prayed, Craig didn't take his or Al's hand. Everything felt too weird at this table. Sitting next to Paisley's father, he eyed the man he'd seen twice at AA meetings. They hadn't spoken about it. But now he figured the liquor he'd found at Paul's house after the hurricane must have been a problem for him. Did anyone else at this table know he attended AA? Craig wouldn't say a word.

Judah and Paisley, sitting across from him, wore pleasant expressions, but he felt unrest within himself every time he met their gazes. While Paisley didn't pelt him with daggers, and even though she politely welcomed Al and him, he recognized fear or mistrust in her gaze. He hated that he caused such feelings. But what could he do about it now?

While Paul was praying, Craig stole a peek around the room. All eyes were closed, other than Piper's. So this was what he missed out on as an only child of a single mother. No fancy Christmas dinners. No kids' table. He glanced over his shoulder. Two boys and Piper sat with Paige, Forest, a silvery-blond woman, and two older adults. Piper grinned at him. He smiled back at her, tempted to wave. No doubt that would be taboo during Christmas Eve grace.

For whatever reason Al agreed to join him, he was thankful he didn't have to face this "family" gathering alone. He'd been planning to take a long beach walk to pass the day away. Since he was avoiding booze, it would have been a long two days of being alone. And if Al hadn't come along, he wouldn't have shown up here either.

Grant blood flowed through his veins, but he knew better than to hope Judah and Paisley, Judah's mom, and this clan might accept him as a real part of their family. They invited him out of a sense of duty or Christian obligation, or whatever. He doubted their sincerity when it came to accepting him for who he was—an offspring of Edward Grant and Evie Masters. Callie Cedars's squinting glare confirmed that.

Paul said, "Amen," then everyone, other than Craig, repeated the word like the end of a coach's pep talk. Dishes and bowls were passed around the table as if it were a synchronized dance. Chatter and laughter followed, sounding like a laughing track on an old TV comedy. Like the noise in Bert's diner, only more subdued.

Paul passed him a pottery bowl of potatoes. "Dish up. Don't be shy." His gaze met Craig's and he nodded as if sending him a message. Maybe encouraging him.

"Uh, thanks." Not hungry, Craig put one scoop on his plate. He passed the bowl to Al. She did a slight eye roll like she was letting him know she'd put up with this shindig, but she didn't like it. He almost chuckled.

"How are you doing with the community service hours?" Paul asked in a pleasant tone and passed him a bowl of gravy.

"Slower than I'd like to get it done."

"No doubt. I never got the chance to express how thankful I am to you for rescuing my girl." Paul nodded toward Paisley who laughed at something with Peter. She met Craig's gaze briefly, then resumed her conversation.

A warmth spread through his chest. He wouldn't call it peace. Relief, perhaps. Thankfully, Paisley was able to act civilly toward him and Al at this table.

"And for keeping Piper and her mama safe." Moisture filled Paul's eyes. "I owe you a world of gratitude. More than you'll ever know."

Craig swallowed. "You're welcome, sir." He glanced at Al. How much had she heard? Her raised eyebrows indicated she heard enough.

Soon their plates were filled. A quiet settled over the room punctuated by the clink of silverware against plates and the occasional chuckle. In the background, instrumental Christmas melodies played.

Al leaned toward him. "You and your brother share one fine quality."

Was she flirting with him? "Good looks and charm?" he bantered back.

"No. That would be two things."

"Right. Then what?"

"Your smile. You both have captivating smiles."

When her lips spread into a pretty smile, something twisted inside him. She was beautiful and witty and charming. He couldn't deny his attraction to her. He was even drawn to her sarcasm and smirky expressions that reminded him of his own. But could this attraction go any further than teasing and the two of them agreeing to get along?

Paisley asked Al a couple of questions, and Craig appreciated her thoughtfulness in including his date in polite conversation. Judah did the same with him. Although a bit awkward, Craig enjoyed being included.

Thoughts of his mom sitting in a jail cell dug at his conscience. She'd made her choices. But he regretted his part in getting her locked up. In grabbing his own freedom at her expense. Although Paul's thanks eased some of his internal pain. Since Edward and Evie were in jail, Paige, Piper, and Paisley were safe. Still, she was his mom.

If Forest hadn't made deals for him with the District Attorney, being included in a family Christmas Eve dinner wouldn't be happening for Craig, either. He'd be in the Basalt Bay jail. Not eating this meal with his new family. Not sitting across from Paisley and Judah. Not sitting next to Al. Not contemplating his next AA meeting where he might have a chat with Paul.

Small blessings.

Some of his tension eased. But didn't his presence stir up bad sentiments in some of the people in this dining room? Callie pegged him with another one of her glares. He almost choked on his bite of roast beef. If he were to stand up and walk out, was there anyone here who wouldn't be relieved to see him go?

Al's expression seemed to say she'd be glad if they did just that.

Forty-nine

The Christmas Eve dinner and cleanup afterward went off without a hitch. Paige was glad there hadn't been any negative talk or contention about newspaper articles, or hers and Paisley's past friendships with Craig, at the dinner table. As far as she knew, no one said anything unkind to Craig and Alison. Even Aunt Callie and Dad co-existed during dinner, although Paige and Paisley purposely situated them at opposite ends of the table.

Even Sarah, sitting between Kathleen and Bess, seemed happy, albeit quiet, during the meal. Was she overwhelmed by so many strangers crammed together in one room? Hopefully, she'd look back on the evening fondly. Paige sure would. Getting to sit by her husband and daughter, and visiting with her sister-in-law, and Forest's mom and dad was a special treat. Taylor and Tommy were fun, lively characters. Piper kept laughing at their antics.

After dinner, Judah gave a short devotional about God's grace and His goodness in their lives. Paige appreciated him taking the lead in bringing their thoughts toward the Lord, reminding them what Christmas was all about.

Now, everyone was congregated in the living room, letting their food settle before dessert was served. Some sat on couches or on the floor. Craig and Alison stood near the big windows. He pointed toward the darkness as if explaining landmarks to her. Even if their being here was a bit awkward, breaking the ice was good for all of them. This might be the way Christmas Eve dinners would be in the future, only with more children added. At least, that's what Paige hoped for.

"Everyone, if I could have your attention!" Judah shouted over the hubbub in the room. "I have an announcement to make."

He did? She watched her brother-in-law, noticing his wide grin. Did he have a gift for Paisley?

"We're going to take a break before we have dessert. Let's call it a Christmas Eve field trip."

Paige met Forest's gaze. "What's going on?"

"Wait and see," he said with a grin.

"We want to invite everyone to jump in your cars and head out to Baker's Point with us." Judah gesticulated as he spoke. "Forest and I have a little surprise."

"Tell me." Paige leaned into Forest's side. "What's this about?"

He kissed her cheek. "Just wait. It's going to be fun." He stood and held out his hand toward her.

Curious, she stood beside him. What was going on at Baker's Point?

The others grabbed coats, shuffling about, and making dibs on the bathrooms. As if they were all in on this, no one questioned Judah's announcement. No one, not even Aunt Callie, bemoaned the weather or having to go outside in the dark on Christmas Eve, which was highly suspicious.

Was she the only one who didn't know what was going on?

Like a Christmas parade, the Cedars and Grant families drove back toward town. At the Baker's Point parking lot, the chilly wind blew hard against her as Paige got out of the car and unfastened Piper from her car seat.

Forest ran around the vehicle. "You trust me, baby, right?" He held up a long piece of narrow black cloth that fluttered in the wind.

"Yes. But what's going on?" She eyed the fabric.

Paisley and Judah jogged over to them.

"Hey, squirt." Judah held out his hands toward Piper.

Laughing and squirming, Piper lunged toward him. Paige let her daughter go to her uncle.

Paisley kissed Paige's cheek. "Merry Christmas, little sister."

"You, too."

Paisley ran after Judah who was galloping down the trail and neighing like a horse with Piper cackling.

"What's happening?" Paige asked Forest.

"I love you."

"Love you too."

He held up the blindfold. "Are you okay with this? I have a surprise for you."

"I guess." She giggled, butterflies dancing up her middle. What kind of surprise required her to wear a blindfold at the beach?

She let Forest tie the fabric strip around her head. Then, leaning into his strong arm, trusting him to keep her from stumbling, she let him lead her down the trail. When they reached the sand and her shoes bogged down in loose grit, a sound foreign to the music of the sea snagged her attention. Was that "The Wedding Waltz?"

"Forest?"

"Just a little ways more."

Pinpricks of light came through the black fabric. Voices and laughter. A cough. The others must already be here.

The blindfold slid off her eyes. The first thing she saw were lanterns and solar lights forming two parallel lines, leading toward—

"Oh, Forest. It's so beautiful."

A new gazebo sat at the end of the aisle of lights. The structure was outlined in tiny lights with white fabric blowing in the breeze at each of the corners. The volume of the music increased. This looked like it was decorated for a—

A wedding?

"Forest, did you build this?"

"Uh-huh. Judah and I did."

"It's amazing." Aww. Had he put their vow renewal together as a surprise Christmas gift for her? Even more love welled in her heart for her husband.

Blankets were spread out on both sides of the line of lights. Teal sat on one with Tommy and Taylor. Bob and Janey sat next to them. Piper was on Judah's lap. Craig and Alison. Peter and Ruby. Dad and James. Aunt Callie, Bess, Kathleen, and Sarah sat on another blanket. Right in front of the gazebo, Pastor Sagle stood, grinning out over his small congregation.

"Merry Christmas, baby!" Forest said.

"It's all so beautiful So perfect." She drew in a breath, taking it all in. He'd done this for her. She and Forest were going to say their vows on Christmas Eve on the beach! "You pulled off a big surprise."

Paisley handed her a bouquet of pink and white roses, baby breath, and deep green foliage. "Surprise!"

"Oh, I am. I'm so shocked, my legs are trembling."

Paisley chuckled. "Just enjoy this."

Clasping Paige's hand, beaming at her, Forest led her down the lighted aisle in the sand until they stood in front of Pastor Sagle.

Before their families and God, with a cool breeze blowing around them in the otherwise still night, Paige and Forest recited their vows to each other again—their third time! Yet, in some ways, beneath the stars and the moon, and with their families present to hear them, it felt like their first time.

When Pastor Sagle told Forest to kiss his bride, the widest grin crossed her husband's face. He took her in his arms and kissed her sweetly. Embracing her more fully, Forest deepened the kiss, tipping her back slightly. Even with the cool sea breeze blowing over them, she felt cocooned in his strong arms, in his love.

Their audience cheered and whistled.

Chuckling, she and Forest ended the kiss. Then, clasping hands, they sang the Doxology acapella with the group. The sea created a glorious background symphony as their voices blended in beautiful unity and praise to God.

Paisley started singing "Silent Night," and everyone joined in. Paige felt such joy at the beauty and sound of their rejoicing on this never-to-be-forgotten Christmas Eve.

Forest giving her this gift of a vow renewal at the new gazebo touched her heart. The ceremony on the beach would be one of the highlight Christmases of her life, something she'd tell her children and grandchildren about someday.

"Happy?" Forest asked her after the song ended. His eyes shining, he leaned closer to her as if waiting eagerly for her answer, or maybe to kiss her.

"So happy. Thank you."

Kissing might have been on his mind, but she met his lips first, hoping her passionate kiss demonstrated how much she loved him. How thankful she was to him for this experience of saying their vows among family and friends.

"Now that's what I call a kiss." He grinned.

"I have an endless supply where that one came from."

"I'm glad to hear it." Forest chuckled in his deep throaty voice. "I'm going to hold you to it."

"Promise?" She snuggled into his arms, enjoying being his bride again.

"I do."

Fifty

As Forest led Paige down the aisle of glowing lights, Paisley stepped into the gazebo, her heart thudding. "May I have your attention?" she called out. "Thank you so much, Judah and Forest, for building this gazebo that will be a blessing to our family, and to the families in our community, for years to come."

"Hear, hear," Aunt Callie hollered.

The group clapped and cheered.

Teal let out a wolf-whistle, which caused some laughter.

"I'm thankful my sister and brother-in-law got to be the first ones to use this gazebo for a vow renewal ceremony. Judah proposed to me the first time right here beneath the timbers of the old gazebo when I was eighteen." She blew him a kiss.

He acted like he caught her kiss against his cheek.

"Judah, would you come up here for a minute?"

Tears flooded her eyes in anticipation of what she was about to tell him, but she fought them.

"Sure." He passed Piper to Forest.

Maybe Paisley should have made this announcement to him privately. But on this monumental Christmas Eve of Paige and Forest's ceremony, and the gazebo's maiden usage, she wanted to tell her husband right here, right now. In fact, she was bursting with the news, if only she could do so and not cave into her emotions.

"What is it?" He approached her grinning.

She kissed his scruffy cheek. Clasping his hands, then moving their fingers so their pinkies linked, she said, "I have something wonderful to share with you in this gazebo you made."

"Another Christmas surprise?"

"Yes, it is."

A few snickers, coughs, and murmurs reached them, but otherwise, their audience was silent, seemingly waiting for her to speak.

As much as she loved her family, Judah was the one who mattered the most in this moment. She withdrew a small, gift-wrapped package from her coat pocket and held it out to him. "Merry Christmas."

"Thank you, sweetheart." He took the package, held it up playfully toward the group, then tore open the Christmas wrap. His gaze flew to hers. "Really? Do you mean it?"

"I really mean it!"

"Oh, Pais." He picked her up and twirled her in a circle, laughing joyously.

She laughed too. Happy tears pooled in her eyes and rolled down her cheeks. Then they kissed, and her tears weren't the only ones mingling on her cheeks.

"Well, what is it?" Aunt Callie called.

"Don't keep us in suspense," Bess said.

Grinning, Judah set Paisley down but kept his arm around her. "This is the best Christmas present I've ever received." He withdrew the pregnancy tester and thrust it into the air. "Paisley and I are going to have a baby!"

"Woohoo!" "Yay!" "Cheers!" "Great news!"

Everyone stood and swarmed them with hugs and congratulations.

"That's what I was hoping for!" Bess clasped Judah's and Paisley's hands. "Congratulations to you both! And to me!" She laughed and hugged them.

After the din died down, Judah put his arm over Paisley's shoulder. "When did you find out?"

"This morning. But I've suspected for two weeks."

"Wow. Are you okay? Any morning sickness?"

"Not yet." She wrapped her arms around his waist. "I'm praying everything goes well this time."

"So will I. We'll pray and believe for that together every day." He kissed her. "This is a sweet surprise, Pais. Thank you."

"For me too." She glanced around at the lights and the gazebo and the family milling about. "This is our first Christmas back together and our first announcement at the gazebo."

"Lots more to come in the future. But we'll always remember this one." He glanced up at the night's sky and mouthed something as if he was saying, "Thank You," to God.

Thank You, she added silently.

Fifty-one

After they put Piper to bed, Paige fixed hot peppermint tea for her and Forest. She handed him a steaming cup, then clasped his hand. "Come with me."

"I'll go anywhere with you, baby."

She smiled, loving her groom's flirtation. She led him to the couch. "I have a surprise for you. Not as grand as your surprise, but one given with all my heart and love."

"Can't wait." He kissed her cheek then sat down.

Paige took a couple of sips of her drink. Setting her mug on a coaster, she turned toward their small tree. A few packages remained beneath the limbs for Piper to open in the morning. Paige leaned behind the tree and pulled out a medium-sized package wrapped in gold paper. Holding Forest's gaze, she shuffled back to him and sat down. "Merry Christmas, my love."

"I like it when you call me sweet names."

He kissed her on the mouth, and she lingered close to him, kissing him back, snuggling against him, loving their time alone together. They were newlyweds, after all.

"You're the best Christmas present I've ever had," he whispered against her cheek.

"Thank you for surprising me with the vow renewal. I still can't believe you did that." She stroked her fingers through his hair, ran her palm down his cheek, so thankful they'd made their way back to each other. They kissed again, slow and delicious. "Now, open your gift." She handed him the package before they could get too distracted.

His eyes sparkled as he peeled off the golden wrapping paper. Finally, he got the box open. His eyes widened as he withdrew three eight-by-ten framed photographs of him and Piper. Paige had repurposed old frames and painted them with chalky black paint, giving them a fresh look.

"Oh, baby. These are amazing. I love them!"

He stared back and forth between the photos. One was of him holding Piper, reading her a story. Paige had taken it on the sly. The other two were of him and Piper playing in the sand on the day of their picnic a month ago. She was pleased with how all three pictures captured the tender expressions on Forest's face, and his care and love for their daughter.

"This was a great day." He tapped the one of him and Piper looking at each other, laughing, playing with the shovel and sand. He met her gaze. "Thank you for these. They're for the mantle, right?"

"Yes." The word caught in her throat. "You'll have some photos of you with Piper to join the others."

"This was sweet of you to make these for me. We should have one of you and me up there too."

"Absolutely. Paisley took some snapshots of us tonight. I'll text her about them."

"That'll be perfect."

Forest strode to the mantle. Paige could have jumped up and helped him rearrange the other pictures, making room for his. Instead, she let him shuffle the frames, placing the photos of him and Piper right where he wanted them.

"Now I feel like I really belong here." He grinned back at her.

"Oh, Forest. You do belong here with Piper and me."

He jogged back and plopped down beside her. In seconds, she was nestled cozily in his arms again. "This has been the best Christmas Eve." He sighed, leaning his head against hers.

"Exciting news about Paisley and Judah having a baby, huh?"

"Yeah. Maybe one of these days we'll have news like that to share too." He touched her cheek.

"I hope so." In fact, she wished she and Paisley could have babies close together. Piper being a little mama to both.

"Do you want to watch a Christmas movie?" he asked.

"I'd like that. What do you think about 'White Christmas?'"

Over the last month, they'd been too busy to watch movies. Since this was their first Christmas together, she didn't even know his likes and dislikes about holiday movies.

"Teal loves it." He chuckled. "Anything is fine with you in my arms. I'm afraid whatever we watch, I might fall asleep."

"Me too." She sighed, feeling tired already.

She clicked the remote and found "White Christmas" in her favorites list. Forest flipped off the lamplight and tugged an afghan over them. They snuggled up together on the couch and watched about fifteen minutes of the movie before he was snoring. She chuckled, but she was nearly asleep too. A few more minutes and she dozed off, thankfulness for their beautiful day filling her heart.

Fifty-two

Early Christmas morning, Peter arrived at the project house and, without knocking, strode into the kitchen that was already beginning to feel like home. Kathleen and Bess worked on something that smelled scrumptiously of ham and cheese and garlic. He couldn't wait to try that dish.

"Good morning!" Bess said.

"Merry Christmas, Peter!" Kathleen grinned.

"Good morning, ladies. Is Ruby around?" He clutched the small package for her behind his back. He'd also hidden an envelope in the interior pocket of his jacket. What would Ruby think of his surprises?

"She hasn't come downstairs yet." Bess lifted a cup. "Want some coffee?"

"Always." He already had plenty at Dad's, but while he waited, he might as well hold a cup and down some more. "Just a sec." He strode into the living room and set the small red package beneath a low-hanging branch of the Christmas tree.

Back in the kitchen, Bess handed him a steaming cup of dark brew. "Creamer's in the fridge."

"I take it black."

"I had a hunch." She pointed toward the island. "There are breakfast rolls and fruit if you're hungry. We'll have the main dish finished soon."

"Sounds good. Thanks." He grabbed one of the rolls shaped like a croissant. "This is great," he said around a mouthful then took a slurp of his coffee to wash it down.

Kathleen beamed. "It's a recipe that's been handed down through my family."

"A spectacular one."

"I thought I heard your voice." Ruby sauntered into the kitchen. "Good morning, Peter."

"Hello, beautiful." He wiped his hand over his mouth and chin bristles.

"You're here early." She yawned. "I just came down for some coffee."

Peter held up his cup. "I beat you to it."

"So I see." She fixed her coffee and set a breakfast roll on a saucer.

In the dining room, she sat down at the corner of the long table with a poinsettia plant in the middle of it. He dropped into the chair beside hers, and they ate their pre-breakfast entrees and drank coffee.

"What would you like to do today?" she asked.

"Spend time with you. I've been remembering a certain secluded porch I'd like to visit again." He winked at her.

"Oh? What exactly did you like about the porch?"

"Kissing. Talking. More kissing." Like magnets, their lips drew together. He kissed her gently. Then pulled back. "Something like that."

"I see what you mean. Visiting on the porch sounds nice."

He was tempted to take her in his arms and plant a doozy of a Christmas kiss on her soft-looking lips. But picturing his aunt walking in and finding him in a make-out embrace with his wife stopped him from doing so.

"If you're game, I'd like us to take a long beach walk." He scooted his chair closer to hers until their knees touched each other's. "I have something special to give you, too."

"I have something for you also."

"My gift is under the tree," he said softly.

She drank from her cup. "I have something under the tree for you, too."

He liked their flirting, sitting together, acting like a romantic couple.

"Rube?" He swept some strands of red hair off her shoulder. "Want to open your present now or later?"

"Now is good." She stood and picked up their dirty dishes. "Let me take care of these first."

He jumped up and helped with carrying their things to the dishwasher, so eager to give Ruby her presents.

In the living room, she sat cross-legged on the floor in front of the Christmas tree. He dropped down beside her, his knees bent, and his arms draped over his kneecaps.

"Merry Christmas." She handed him a wrapped box.

He reached for the red package he set beneath the tree earlier. "Merry Christmas," he said as he handed it to her.

"Oh, Peter, it's lovely."

He chuckled. "You've only seen the wrapping."

"I know. But it's pretty. Why don't you go first?" She nodded toward the package he held.

He tugged the paper off the foot-long square box which had some weight to it. Ruby was half grinning and half gnawing on her lower lip as if she were nervous. But there he was staring at her lips.

"Open it."

"Can't a guy enjoy watching his wife?"

"Yes, he can," she whispered.

Unable to resist kissing her, he brushed his mouth against hers. They smiled at each other.

He sighed and tugged open the box, recognizing the fishing gear he'd ogled at the hardware store in Ketchikan. "Oh, wow." He withdrew one of those newfangled sonar gizmos. "This is great. Thanks, Rube." He nodded toward the package clutched in her hands. "Your turn."

She opened the package slowly, glancing back and forth between it and him. If only he brought a dozen packages so he could enjoy the sweet look on her face for a long time. Of course, he still had the envelope in his pocket. He smoothed his hand over the fabric to check. Still there.

When Ruby opened the small necklace box, she drew in a sharp breath. "Oh, Peter, it's exquisite." She pulled up the gold chain and dangled the ruby between them.

"Like it?"

"I love it. But it's too expensive. How can we afford it?"

"Don't worry about that. I wanted to give you something special."

"It really is." She unclasped the chain and held it out to him. "Help me with it, will you?"

"Sure." His fingers fumbled with the small clasp. Working around her hand holding up her hair, he fidgeted with the clasp until it finally fastened. "There."

She dropped her hair down. "Thank you. The necklace is the most beautiful gift I've ever received."

"You're welcome." He took her hand in his and settled closer to her. He liked how she leaned against him, too. "I got it before I came to Basalt Bay looking for you the first time."

"You did?"

"I planned to give it to you then, but I left due to the storm."

"Oh, right. So you got this when you spoke to Stacy?"

"Yes. A ruby for my Ruby."

"Thank you for such a wonderful gift. I don't mean only the necklace." She fingered the jewel. "I mean you being here. What you said to me yesterday. The way you've been holding me close like this. Being more open with me. Even saying I'm your Ruby."

"Ah, Rube, you are mine. I like holding you close." He touched his mouth to hers, lingering, deepening their kiss.

"Breakfast is ready!" Kathleen called from the doorway. "Oops. Sorry."

Ruby pulled back, her face reddening. "That's okay, Kathleen."

Peter snickered.

The older woman hollered, "Callie, Sarah, breakfast is served!" Then she shuffled back the way she came, chuckling.

Peter stood, bringing Ruby with him. If he could have one wish granted, it would be for her to stay in his arms for the rest of the day. "There is one other thing I want to give you today."

"What's that?"

He loved how her eyes shimmered up at him. How she smiled at him as if she loved him deeply. Withdrawing the envelope from his jacket, he held it out to her. "Merry Christmas, Rube."

"You already gave me a fantastic present." Glancing at him, she tore open the envelope. "Peter—" She stared at the printout he copied. "Are you kidding me?"

"Not kidding."

She lunged into his arms. "Are you sure?"

"I'm sure I want us to be together. In a boat, on land, in Alaska, or here, it's you and me. That's what matters."

It looked like she was going to kiss him, but then, Aunt Callie's bedroom door opened.

"Peter. Ruby."

"Merry Christmas, Aunt Callie."

"Same to you." His aunt shuffled through the room, glancing suspiciously at them over her shoulder.

Ruby snuggled against him, holding out the photocopy of a small house in Ketchikan. Aloud, she read his hand-written note. "'Whenever you're ready to head north with me, we'll look at as many houses as you'd like until we find the perfect one for us. Then we'll buy it together. Yours, Peter.'" She smiled at him. "This means a lot to me."

"There's no pressure to rush back. If you'd rather live here, it would mean us traveling back and forth to be there for the fishing openings, but we could make it work. Us being together. That's what I want. What I hope you want too." He wrapped his arms fully around her, tugging her back against him. He decided to take another swing at being honest. "However, I am hoping we can get back together soon."

"Soon as in here?" She turned in his arms, gazing at him. "Like us staying together?"

He nodded slowly. "Would you let me stay with you, Rube?" She didn't answer, so he kept speaking. "For us to keep working stuff out, talking and sharing, and, well, doing husband and wife things." He grinned at the sweet woman in his arms, praying she was ready for what he was proposing. "You left, so it's up to you to come back to me. Or for you to invite me to come home to you. But, yes, I am asking if I can move in with you." Hoping he wasn't pushing her too quickly, he kissed her gently. "Just in case I haven't been clear enough, I'd like to be your husband in every way."

Their lips met again.

Suddenly, she pulled back, looking dazed, uncertain. "I like us being close. I'm just—"

"What?"

"Confused. And a little enamored with you."

He chuckled "I'm enamored with you also." But he wasn't confused. He loved Ruby and wanted to be her husband for the rest of his life. Instead of kissing her again, he hugged her, holding her gently. "I love you so much."

"I love you."

Hearing her say the words made him feel whole. Them moving back in together was still on his mind, but more than anything, he wanted the privilege of being with her like this for as long as he could.

Fifty-three

All through Christmas breakfast, Ruby and Peter exchanged glances. Did he want to head out to the porch and "talk" some more? Ruby felt like they were teenagers sitting at their parents' table but silently communicating with each other about sneaking away and kissing. Whenever she thought of the things he said to her this morning, her heart pounded furiously. Move back in together? Was she ready for that? Did he mean today?

Getting back together meant more than sneaking him up to her attic bedroom. It meant sharing their lives, their whole lives, and it meant agreeing to go back to Alaska to work on the troller with him, too. Was she ready for that?

He had sweetly apologized for his previous neglect. He seemed sincere about his spiritual and emotional metamorphosis. He was talking with her more. But she needed to know he'd be her confidant in every aspect of their lives. Not just the things pertaining to their world as fishermen. Would they fall back into their old routines too easily?

She met his gaze in between bites of the yummy egg dish Bess and Kathleen prepared. Was he willing to step up and be a real partner with her? He mentioned taking a walk. That might be a good time to work out more of the questions she had.

She zeroed in on a childhood story Sarah was telling. Something about her grandmother serving salmon and lobster for Christmas dinner. It was nice seeing her being more relaxed and enjoying herself. What Sarah had told her about wishing an argument hadn't been the last interaction between her and her husband had really spoken to Ruby's heart.

She wanted to make her relationship right with Peter. What would sharing the attic space with him be like? Would that even be okay with the other ladies?

Peter smiled at her and clasped her hand beneath the table like he did yesterday. She was so attracted to him. Was he serious about starting a family?

He leaned toward her and whispered, "You okay?"

"I'm all right. Just processing."

"Any chance of us sorting things out together?"

"I'd like that. Later?"

He nodded.

His wanting to keep talking with her was some of the husband and wife stuff she wanted more of. Of course, she couldn't deny she was looking forward to more of his kisses too.

Fifty-four

Craig stared into his coffee mug, trying to ignore the strains of "Jingle Bells" playing in Bert's diner. Since it was Christmas morning, this should be the last time he had to endure the holiday song for the next ten months. Tomorrow the place would be back to its usual 50s and 60s tunes.

Fortunately, Bert had kept the joint open for the breakfast crowd who didn't have family to celebrate with or for those who chose to spend the day alone. Maggie Thomas sat in a window seat. Farther down the line, C.L. hunched over a newspaper. James Weston sat at the breakfast bar drinking coffee.

Where was Mia? She was usually flitting about the room, flirting with any takers. He hadn't seen her all week. She didn't answer any of his recent texts. Maybe she was avoiding him.

He'd bet she was the one who fed Al, or her uncle, the garbage about Forest. But why was she still listening to whatever bunk Edward coerced her into doing? Since he was in jail, and most likely heading to prison, it wasn't like he could come through on his promises, or his threats.

Evie had hinted at someone else's involvement in her and Edward's plans, but she never revealed the person to him. Was it Mia? Was she as power hungry as Edward? Or did she just get caught up in his web of lies the way Craig did?

He raked his fingers through his hair.

Lucy stopped by his table. "Ready to order?"

"Yeah. Short stack. More coffee."

"You got it." She bent closer to his ear. "I'm about to take a break. Mind if I join you?"

He almost agreed, but the bell jangled. Al sauntered inside the diner. Their gazes met.

"Not this time."

"I didn't know you were meeting *her*."

Neither did he.

Huffing, Lucy bustled away.

Al sauntered over to his table, a smile on her red lips. Craig stood. Good thing he wasn't wearing his fluorescent jail vest today. He smoothed his hands down his light blue button-up shirt, feeling more human, more like a decently-dressed man a woman like Al might care to be interested in. "Al."

"I told you—"

"Want to share my table?" His heart felt lighter. Having someone to share the space with on Christmas Day made his life seem not so lonely or pathetic. Although Lucy made her offer plain enough.

"Okay. Thanks." His plus-one from yesterday dropped into the chair across from him.

He lowered himself to his seat. "I'm surprised to find you here this morning."

"Thought I had big plans, did you?" She chuckled. "After yesterday's fiasco, I might need a week's rest."

"Me too. All that noise and chaos."

"All those people crammed into one room." She sighed like she didn't really mean what she said.

Maybe she enjoyed the pleasure of a family gathering. No one acting like they hated him or her.

"Coffee?" Lucy buzzed back to their table and set a mug down in front of Al.

"Yes. Thank you."

"Are you staying in Basalt?" Lucy poured the hot coffee. "Or just filling time until Milton gets back?"

Craig squinted at her, trying to warn her to back off.

"It's temporary. I haven't heard from—" Al shrugged. "Never mind."

Lucy gazed at Craig for a few awkward seconds then zoomed off again.

"Was she staking her territory?" Al quirked an eyebrow.

"Beats me. She invited herself to sit with me."

"I bet she did." Al cut him a cute grin. "If I was a server in this sad, lonely hearts' club on Christmas morning, I'd ask to sit with a handsome man like you, too."

Her full-on smile aimed at him took his breath away. Getting women like Lucy or Mia to smile at him didn't take much effort. Al smiling at him? Acting like she might be interested in him as more than a plus-one? He'd do whatever it took to get that expression on her face more often. In fact, he liked her mouth a lot. Probably shouldn't be staring at it. Did she call him handsome?

"What did you think of the Cedars-Grant bash yesterday?" she asked. "Not one of them, not even Callie, blasted me about my articles. I caught the old gal glaring at me a couple times, but she didn't say a word. Neither did Forest. I was almost disappointed."

"Think they made a group decision to not discuss anything negative?"

"Maybe. Should I expect them to line up at my office Monday morning?"

"Could be." He chuckled.

"I'll Be Home for Christmas" played from Bert's sound system. The front door opened a couple more times. Craig guzzled a few swigs of his coffee.

Lucy stopped by their table and faced Al, ordering pad at the ready. "What will it be?"

"Number"—Al winked at Craig—"Five."

Lucy's jaw dropped. "Again?"

Craig guffawed.

Lucy nearly ran away from their table.

Al leaned toward him. "I did that to make you laugh."

"Oh, yeah?" A powerful attraction for her hit him. Her soft red lips looked so inviting, especially when she smiled at him like she was doing now. They were much too different, or maybe too alike, to ever make a go of it. But something drew him to her like a moth to light. "It'll be the highlight of my day to watch you clean your plate."

Al chuckled. "I can't eat so much and keep my waist trim.

But it's Christmas. I'm sitting across from a nice, handsome man. Why not celebrate?"

Nice and handsome, huh?

"Why not, indeed?" The strongest urge to clasp her hand came over him. Maybe to tug her fingers to his mouth and kiss them one by one. What would she say if he did?

They sipped their coffees and talked about mundane things. But each minute spent with Al fanned Craig's hope like a wilting fire coming back to life under a gentle wind. Were he and Al attracted to each other enough to start a relationship? What would she say if he asked her out on a real date?

Lucy dropped a short stack of pancakes in front of him and set a plate in front of Al that looked mounded even higher than the previous one she'd ordered. Craig almost guffawed again, but the sparkly-eyed gaze of the beautiful woman sitting across from him set his heart on fire, stopping any mocking laughter from spewing out of his mouth.

Something untamed and powerful, like a wildfire in a tinder-dry forest, was happening between them. Maybe something sweet and spicy like he hadn't experienced in a long time. Whatever it was, he wanted to bask in this aura of being with a woman who liked him, and one whom he liked a whole lot, even if it was only for this one day.

Fifty-five

Ruby clasped Peter's hand as they strolled away from the project house, heading south of town. Thanks to the low tide, they could walk for a long way before they'd be forced to turn back.

"This has been a nice Christmas weekend," he said. "I'll never forget it."

"Me neither."

As they hiked, Peter wasn't chatty, which was okay. She didn't expect him to change his personality or the way he thought deeply about things before speaking. But there was something she needed to hear from him before she'd seriously consider them getting back together, maybe even today.

"Peter?"

"Hmm?" He swung their clasped hands between them and smiled. She loved how he was smiling at her more.

"You know what you said about us moving in together?" She decided to get right to the heart of the matter.

"Yes." Eyebrows raised, he stopped walking but kept his hand linked with hers. "What do you think about that? Is it too soon?"

"You said there weren't any strings attached."

"That's right."

"But in a way there are. While living together, sleeping together, sounds good, and I want to be with you too," she added softly, "I'm worried about the other parts of our lives. Like working together on the boat, and possibly reverting to us not focusing on our marriage. Even buying a house could have its tough moments between us."

"Sure. I get that." He let go of her hands and ran both of his palms down her shoulders and back, still gazing deeply into her eyes, her heart, it seemed. "But I promise you I'm all in. You matter to me. My heart is yours, Rube." He took a breath. "I want us to work together on the boat as partners. Co-captains, if you will."

"Co-captains, Peter?"

Could he ever put down the mighty control he had when his boat and fishing were involved?

"I mean it! I promise you I mean it." His face flushed red. In his burly voice, he asked, "Will you be my co-captain on the *Lily Forever*, in buying a house, in having a family with me?" His tone went quiet. "Please, Rube, will you be mine?"

Tears—*tears*—flooded Peter's eyes.

Her heart melted. "You really want us to have kids now?"

"Yes."

She gulped. She would not cry ugly tears on Christmas Day. But they were so close to spilling out.

"When Judah announced they were having a baby"—Peter smoothed his hands over hers—"I longed to hear those words from you. I want us to be a family. You, me, and whatever kiddos we have."

Stepping back, he gazed at her with wide, clear eyes which seemed to proclaim he was telling her the complete truth, not just telling her what she wanted to hear to make peace.

"Co-captains, huh?"

"If that doesn't prove my love to you, I don't know what does."

"Then I accept!" She laughed. "Yes, I will be your co-captain. On the boat, in our home, in our family, and in our lives together."

Then she was in his arms, kissing him, him kissing her, and her whole being felt infused with heat and love for this man. When they finally broke apart, although Peter still held her close, a thought came to mind, and she knew what she wanted to say.

"Would you be willing to exchange vows with me?"

A slight frown crossed his features. "Like Paige and Forest did last night?"

"Yes. But just us, privately."

He sighed like he was relieved to hear that. "Sure. Right here? Now?"

"Yes." She chuckled at his sudden enthusiasm.

"How do you want to do this?"

"How about if I start since it was my idea?" She clasped his cool hands and gazed into his shining eyes. "I love you, Peter. I've missed being with you since I left. I'm sorry my leaving hurt you. But I'm glad it led to this. To us. I'd like to pledge myself to you again right now."

He kissed her as if she'd finished with her vows. She enjoyed the kiss, letting the emotion and love she felt for him roll over her like a giant wave, but she wanted to say more.

"Okay. Okay." She pushed him back slightly. "Let me finish. I, Ruby Cedars, take you, Peter Cedars, to be my husband for the rest of my life. I choose you to be the one I talk to as my closest confidant, the man I want to share my life with, the one who I want to hold for all our nights."

"Oh, Rube." He tugged her into his arms again.

"Wait. I promise to stay with you, love you, share experiences, and"—she grinned—"kiss you every day for as long as I live."

She kissed him like a couple on their honeymoon to prove her point.

"Okay. My turn." Peter cleared his throat. "Rube, you are my favorite person in the whole world. Without you, I've felt a chunk of me was missing. I never want to feel that way again. I love you so much." He drew in a long breath. "I, Peter Cedars, take you, Ruby Cedars, as my wife for the rest of my days. I promise to talk to you every day as my closest friend and ally, as if you are a part of my heart ... because you are."

Tears invaded her eyes, making seeing him difficult.

"I failed at being a good husband in the past. But before God and you, I pledge to be a better man for you. A good father to our children. I love you, now and forevermore." He took on a playful tone. "You may kiss your bride!"

His lips fell across hers in a beautiful, hot, passionate exchange of promises and love. They kissed and clung to each other. Then kissed some more.

All the way back to the project house, they talked and shared their hopes and dreams. They took turns describing what kind of house each of them would like, how many children they hoped to have, and taking guesses about what the upcoming fishing season might be like.

It was a perfect Christmas walk. And as Ruby led Peter up the ship's ladder to her attic space, she knew it was just the beginning of something delightful between them.

Fifty-six

Ali didn't know why she agreed to go for a beach walk with Craig. Hadn't she spent enough time with the dark-eyed, brooding man she previously dubbed as trouble? She didn't want to stir something up with him. So what was she doing getting ready to meet him again?

She and Craig were night and day. Ice and fire. Yet there was something compelling in those stark differences. A megawatt magnetic pull lured her toward him like no other man ever had. But what about her going back to Portland? What if she got all into him, then they broke up because long-distance relationships never worked?

Her cell phone rang. "Milton" displayed on the screen.

"Uncle Milton, merry Christmas!"

"Alison," he said in a somber tone. "Not so merry, I'm afraid."

"What's wrong?" She held the phone tighter to her ear. "Are you coming home soon?"

"I can't do that."

"Why not? Are you okay?"

"I may have to sell … the paper," he barked out in phrases.

"What? Why?"

"I can't discuss it on the phone." He inhaled sharply. "Some wrongs follow a man to his death."

"What's going on? Are you sick?"

"Sick at heart. On the run. I know things—" He groaned. "You have questions I can't answer."

"Of course, I have questions. I'm a reporter! Uncle Milton, please, tell me what's going on."

"I want you to put out tomorrow's paper, shut off the lights, and walk away."

"But—"

"I mean it. I should never have dragged you into my mess, into the town's mess. You've done your best. But things are about to—" A silence. "Promise me you'll leave town."

"What mess are you talking about? What's about to happen? None of this makes sense!"

"Just get out of Basalt Bay and don't look back!"

She tensed. He'd never spoken to her so sharply before.

"Where are you?"

"I can't say."

"Uncle Milton, let's face this together. We're family."

"I don't want you involved. Leave town ASAP!"

She wasn't a child for him to tell her what to do. "I'm not running." She almost blurted, "like you," but didn't. What was someone holding over him to make him become a fearful shell of the man he used to be? What did he know that was so secretive?

"If I testify at the trial, something might happen," he said quietly.

"If?"

"I'm being watched. This call might be compromised. They might come after you next."

"Who?" Rushing over to the window, Ali peered outside. An older couple walked past and gazed at her. Not in a malicious way. More like curiously. Was Uncle Milton just being paranoid?

"I'm going to ditch this phone. Get another one."

"You're scaring me. Go to the police!"

"You don't know how far Edward's—" Uncle Milton coughed. "Have you been harassed by anyone?"

"Hate mail and glares. Nothing I can't handle."

"I shouldn't have given you those assignments. Please, be careful."

"It's what we do. We pursue the truth." Doubts others had mentioned came to mind. "You were confident of your source about Forest Harper, right?" Another silence. "Uncle Milton? You checked and approved your source, right?"

She sat in the same room as Forest did during yesterday's dinner. She listened to him saying his vows to Paige on the beach, his teary eyes speaking of his sincerity and love. He gently held their daughter and was loving and kind to his parents, sister, and nephews. Things a nice guy would do. How could he be the troublemaker the source claimed he was?

"I can't explain." Uncle Milton gulped. "If things don't end well ... if I don't see you again, I've always loved you."

"Uncle Milton!"

"Some people in Basalt Bay—" He mumbled something. "It's better if you don't know what's about to happen. Just go back to Portland. Live your life."

"What's about to happen? Who gave you the information about Forest?"

"I can't reveal my source. If you knew what I do, you'd leave today."

She had never run from a story before. Wouldn't now.

"Have you heard anything about Mike Linfield leaving C-MER?"

His off-subject question jammed up her train of thought. Who? Linfield. Oh, right. His name showed up in the documents concerning the dike.

"What about him?" She rushed to the desk and jotted the man's name down on a notepad.

"If you're determined to stay, investigate why he left. Keep a low profile. Stay safe, Alison."

She ignored his warning. "So this guy left C-MER suddenly?"

"That's right."

"About the same time you left the newspaper office?" She took a guess.

"I have to go. Be safe."

"You, too. Keep in touch."

The call ended.

Ali groaned and dropped onto her chair. She had fifteen minutes until she and Craig were supposed to meet. Yet she felt so troubled and anxious for her uncle.

Did Mike Linfield and Uncle Milton leave town around the same time? Was he serious about her possibly being in danger? What if she'd been used like a pawn to get back at Forest for something unjustified? Or to weaken the case against Edward?

A fury ignited within her. She would not sit on this. No one was stopping her from pursuing the truth and doing her job!

Fifty-seven

Craig paced back and forth along the shoreline at City Beach, waiting for Al to show up. It wasn't like her to be late. Was she standing him up? So much for his daydreams about her and him possibly starting a relationship.

She was big city. He was small potatoes. She normally worked in Portland. He was a criminal serving time in Basalt Bay. He wasn't the most trustworthy guy in town. He had a past. Offenders for parents. It might take some doing to convince her, or any woman, to take a chance on him. But something about Al made him want to persuade her to do just that.

Hands tucked into his jacket pocket, he turned toward the sea, breathing in the salty air. The talk Judah gave yesterday after dinner swirled through his brain. What did he call it? A devotion. At first, he'd been annoyed by Judah's topic. Stuff about God's love changing the hardest of hearts. Did he mention grace and forgiveness for Craig's benefit? Maybe Al's?

But then, when he recalled some things he heard Judah say before, his snide attitude dissipated. Once at C-MER, he'd overheard Judah telling some guys that all they had to do was accept Jesus and their lives would be changed. He seemed to believe that stuff.

What did it all mean, anyway? God's love. God's grace. Accept Him. Code words for Christianity?

Surely, just accepting what Jesus did was too simple. There had to be something else. Like his community service requirements demanded action of him, didn't he have to do penance or jail time to make up for his sins?

He groaned. Why was he even thinking about such heavy topics on Christmas Day?

"Craig." Al's voice.

He turned and watched her saunter toward him. Her long blondish hair floated on a gust of wind. He loved her hair hanging loose, moving in unison with her body. He loved her almost-smile as if she was holding herself back from giving him a full smile, which only made him want to make her smile more. There was something mysterious about her that invited him to try to get to know her better.

"Hey, Al."

"I wore my hiking boots." She lifted one booted foot. "Not my style."

He laughed. "Care for a Christmas hike?"

"Why not? I could use some wind blowing the cobwebs out of my brain."

When she linked her hand into the crook of his arm, he felt lighthearted and energized, as if he could skim over the sand like a surfer riding a wave. He synced his stride with hers and walked along the north shoreline beside her. If anyone saw them together, they might assume they were a couple. But who in their right mind would want him for a boyfriend?

A flash of Paisley's smiling face crossed his memory. She'd been kind and welcoming toward him and Al yesterday. The perfect hostess. But when Judah made the announcement out at the gazebo about him and her having a baby, Craig felt cut to the quick with jealousy. He could barely breathe for a few seconds. His brother and sister-in-law's happiness and love were so obvious between them. Regrets over the way he'd coveted another man's wife in the past scorched his conscience. He'd certainly made his share of mistakes.

He shot a glance at Al. Saw her slight smile aimed at him. And everything in his heart momentarily aligned. He needed to let the past go. Let all those old feelings die. Maybe then he might stand a chance with someone like Al.

Judah said people could start over. Begin fresh with God. Was that true? Craig could use a fresh start. A reason to live. If only—

"You're quiet."

"Sorry. I've been chewing on Judah's after-dinner chat."

"About love and such?"

"Yeah."

Their gazes met. It wasn't like them to discuss deeper stuff. Thus far, their conversations had mostly been shallow and mocking. Their dry sense of humor was something else they had in common. Honesty and vulnerability were tougher ponds to skate on.

"And about God. Grace, too."

"Well, it is Christmas." She glanced toward the sky. "If any time is a good time to consider spiritual topics, it's now, don't you think?"

Her sincerity surprised him.

"Maybe. Do you ever ponder such things?" He wasn't trying to be pushy. More like questioning everything.

"Sure. I went to Sunday school and youth camp as a kid."

"Grew up and became hard-nosed, huh?" he said, keeping things light.

"Something like that. And you?"

"No Sunday school or church."

"Yet you're focusing on it now." She tugged on his arm. "Why?"

He led her around a large rock, avoiding the muddiest places on the beach. He liked not having to slow down for her to keep up with him. ·

"Some of the family have been kind to me, even when"—hard for him to admit—"I wasn't exactly pleasant to them."

"You have a past with them, don't you?"

"It's a long story."

Since she was a newspaper reporter, there were things he'd rather not talk about with her. If the past could be done away with as Judah said, Craig wouldn't mind finding out how. Sometimes the guilt he carried nearly suffocated him. He wouldn't want Al writing about his past, broadcasting his faults like she did with Forest.

"We have time to talk if you want."

Her alluring smile made him want to move closer to her. Yet there was a strain around her eyes. Hadn't she gotten a good night's sleep? Was she working too much?

"Some things are better kept to myself." Hopefully, she didn't take offense.

"I understand."

They walked farther down the beach, passing the C-MER building, bypassing tidal pools, keeping ahead of the waves coming in, laughing over nonsensical things. Being with Al felt good. Only he couldn't help wishing for something more than friendship. But if that's all he could have with her, he'd take it, for now.

"May I tell you something?" she asked as they headed back toward City Beach. "You can't mention it to anyone. But it's bugging me like crazy."

"Okay." Who would he tell anyway?

"My uncle wants me to shut down the newspaper and leave town."

His heart lurched. He wasn't in love with her, but he'd hate it if she suddenly left.

"Why?"

"It's private. Newspaper stuff." She tugged on the edge of his sleeve. "This may sound weird, but I'm not ready to leave."

"I don't want you to leave, either." He swallowed with effort, forcing out the words, "I'm here if you need anything. Basalt Bay has its challenging people, but I hope you'll stay. Work through whatever difficulties you may be having."

"Thank you." She kissed his cheek. She was just being friendly, but he was tempted to turn and meet her red lips he'd been dying to taste.

They weren't in a relationship, so he didn't try anything. He didn't have a right to start something with her he couldn't continue, especially if she might be leaving town soon. But still, the yearning for something more with her, maybe something long-lasting, persisted.

Fifty-eight

"How did you feel toward Craig yesterday?" Judah asked Paisley as they sat relaxing together on the couch.

She'd thought he might ask her about that subject last night when they got home, but he didn't. After all the excitement with Paige and Forest's vow renewal, Paisley's surprise about the baby, and even getting through the awkwardness around Craig and Al, they were too exhausted to talk about anything else. She'd fallen right to sleep.

Earlier, they ate breakfast on the veranda, but since the air was cool outside, they came back inside for their second cup of coffee. Then they exchanged gifts.

Judah gave her a beautiful journal and pen. He said writing down her thoughts during the upcoming trial might be good for her. He also gave her a gift card to buy new clothes, something she was genuinely going to need for maternity wear. She gave him a new tool belt and for fun, a cute plaque with "hot husband" displayed on it.

Now, his arms surrounded her, and she rested her cheek against his chest, her head rising and falling with his breathing. It was nice just to relax together.

"Pais?"

Oh, right. She hadn't answered. "When I look at him, I still think of some things I'd rather not remember. But I'm thankful too. He rescued me from Edward. He helped my dad. The rest? I want to put it behind us. I have forgiven him."

"Me too. I'm proud of the way you held your composure, were kind to him and his guest. Thank you for doing that."

"Of course." She met his lips in a warm kiss. "With you by my side, I can face anything." She smoothed her hand over her flat stomach. "All the other stuff doesn't compare to what I have in my life now. Why hold onto any of it?"

"Exactly. I was amazed by your news." He settled his hand over hers. "We're going to be parents. You, me, and baby will make three."

She chuckled at his rhyme. "I'm so happy."

"We'll never forget Misty Gale. But I can't wait to hold this little one."

She took a deep breath, thankful he still thought of their firstborn too. "We'll have to figure out names. Although, we have plenty of time."

"What do you want? A boy or a girl?"

"A boy with beautiful blue eyes like you." She kissed his scruffy cheek. "And your nice smile."

"Or a girl with long dark hair and matching eyes. One who gets into mischief like her mama does."

"Hey. My mischief-making days are over."

"Right." He laughed like he didn't believe her.

They sat quietly, cuddled close.

"What do you want to do today?" He ran his fingers down her arm. "Last night was the big to-do with the family. We can do anything we want today."

"I'd like to take a beach hike, even though it's chilly."

"We can bundle up. I'll keep you warm." He wrapped his arms fully around her again and closed his eyes. "A nap sounds good too."

"Hey. I'm the one who gets the naps now."

"Aw, come on. Dads get tired too."

"I like that."

"What?" He opened his eyes and stared at her with a lazy look.

"Dad."

He pressed his mouth softly against hers, his kiss slow and deliciously sweet, and she melted into his embrace.

His phone buzzed. Groaning, he picked it up and stared at the screen. "Craig." He held his phone out to her so she could read the text.

Can we meet up?

"I wonder what this is about," Judah said.

Paisley too, the next text said.

"Why does he want to see me?"

"I don't know. Do you think we should? I mean, it sounds like he's reaching out."

She wouldn't stand in the way of Judah and Craig trying to mend their relationship. "Do whatever you think is best."

He typed, *Okay. Meet at Bert's?*

Or City Beach? Craig texted back.
"Is this okay with you?" Judah asked her.
"I think so."
It would be okay, right?

Fifty-nine

Craig kicked the toe of his shoe against a mound of sand. Asking Judah and Paisley to meet him on Christmas afternoon might have been a ridiculous request. Hadn't he crashed into their lives enough yesterday?

Would apologizing to Paisley and Judah make anything better? Or would trying to make amends stir the pot of hurt feelings about the past even more?

He'd been to a handful of AA meetings. Heard people give testimonials about their habits and their journey back from the abyss. He carried the card with the twelve steps in his wallet. Had read Step Nine about a hundred times. He dreaded the part about making amends with people.

But this wasn't about him taking a certain step. He had to make things right with Paisley and Judah for himself, because he needed to say the words. No more faking it. No more pretending to be family with them. After yesterday, he wanted brotherhood with Judah and all that entailed, including being invited to future holiday dinners. But only after, and if, they cleared the air.

But today? Why had he stupidly texted them about meeting him on Christmas Day?

Maybe he should shoot Judah another text and say he changed his mind. *Something came up. Let's meet up in ten years.* What happened in the past should stay in the past. Why drudge it up?

He paced back and forth across the sand, tempted to keep walking. But he couldn't escape his blame over past wrongs. He was the flake who went along with Edward's demands. The same way others in the ex-mayor's circle had done. Probably the same way Mia was doing now. He thought of the newspaper articles Al wrote. Was she listening to Edward, too?

"Craig." Judah's voice.

He turned and saw his brother's hand raised in a wave. He waved back. Felt a tightening in his chest. Over the past month, he'd done a lot of humbling things—picking up trash, wearing the glaring green vest, talking about his weaknesses in AA. Facing Judah and Paisley, and the guilt of his previous actions, was like a summons on his spirit that he couldn't move forward until he did.

"Merry Christmas," Judah said and shook his hand.

Paisley, standing beside Judah, looked tense, almost fearful. What could he say to make things better? How could he erase that mistrust from her eyes?

"Merry Christmas," he said haltingly. "Thanks for including Al and me in yesterday's festivities. You were both nice to us. I appreciate that more than I can say."

"Sure," Judah said. "Great day for a beach walk, huh?"

"A bit breezy." What was he doing discussing the weather? "Look, you're probably shocked by my request to meet up."

"Is there something you need? Something we can help with?"

It was just like Judah to offer kindness or friendship right off. Craig sighed, the heaviness of what he needed to say pressing on his chest like a rock being shoved into his ribs.

"I wanted to meet with you, um, both to say"—he forced himself to meet Paisley's gaze, to not look away—"I'm sorry for what happened between us three years ago. For what I set into motion." Feeling such anguish in his gut over this confession, and over his wrongs, he thought he might be sick. Paisley looked equally ill at ease. "Paisley, my pursuing you was wrong when you were still married to Judah. I'm sorry for doing that. For any harm my actions caused."

Her eyes widened, but she didn't glance away from him. Didn't act like she despised him, either. That gave him courage to continue.

"I never should have tried anything. I apologize to both of you for my stupidity. I just—" He lifted then dropped his hands. "I could blame Edward all day long, but I was at fault too. I'm so sorry." He shrugged. "That's what I wanted to say."

Paisley nodded and blinked fast.

"Judah, you were a friend. I should never have gone after your woman." This time he held out his hand toward him. "Can you forgive me for acting so rude? So, uh, wretchedly idiotic?"

"Yes, of course." His brother didn't hesitate. He clasped Craig's hand, then clapped him on the back in a brief hug.

"Thanks, man. Apologizing takes courage." He put his arm over Paisley's shoulder and tugged her against his side. "We both appreciate your saying this."

The tender move was possessive and loving at the same time. Craig got the message loud and clear—Judah and Paisley were together, married, and always would be. He'd circumspectly honor that in the future.

Paisley wiped her fingers beneath her eyes as if she was fighting being emotional. She took a step away from Judah, her gaze locked on his. An unspoken dialogue seemed to pass between them.

She reached out her hand toward Craig. It felt like a lifeline was tossed to a drowning victim—him drowning in misery and regret, and her saving him. Once, he rescued her. Now, they were even.

He clasped her hand and held it gently.

"I forgive you, Craig," she said softly.

That knot of guilt and regret that had been strangling his neck for as long as he could remember melted. Forgiveness was a beautiful, undeniable gift he didn't deserve. But he embraced it with all he had in him.

"Thank you." He took a deep breath and blinked fast, unfamiliar with the tears filling his eyes. "Your forgiveness means everything to me."

She released his hand and stepped back to Judah. Their hands found each other's.

Craig longed for the beautiful relationship these two had discovered. If that kind of love was possible for him someday, he had just the woman in mind—one with long blond hair, blue eyes, and great legs.

"On our way over here, Paisley and I were talking about building a bonfire on the beach in front of our cabin tonight. Making s'mores. Singing carols. Would you and Alison be interested in joining us? You'd be welcome."

Judah's invitation surprised him. "Sure. I can't agree for Al, but I'll ask her."

"Perfect. Let's say seven?"

After shaking Craig's hand again, Judah led Paisley back along the beach the way they came.

Craig stood watching them depart, but for the first time in a long time, he didn't feel lonely or jealous of them.

Sixty

Ali didn't know why she agreed to go on another outing with Craig. A Christmas bonfire with him, Judah, and Paisley? How absurd. Yet here she was holding a stick over the fire with a golden marshmallow dangling off the end, enjoying herself. Her concerns about Uncle Milton weren't far from her thoughts, but she was trying to let the weight of them go until tomorrow.

A plan was already formulating in her mind for getting to the bottom of her uncle's disappearance. She wouldn't stop until she found out where he was and what he thought was going to happen to the town.

Craig laughed with Judah over something concerning their old jobs. A shared memory.

She watched him in profile, a hitch catching in her throat when he met her gaze. His dark eyes glowed toward her like burning coals in the firelight. Some of that intoxicating allurement she experienced earlier rushed through her again.

She liked how relaxed he was tonight. How he smiled and laughed easily. What transpired between their walk and this evening to cause such a look of happiness on his face? His casual stance, the way he didn't appear to mind being around his brother and sister-in-law, the way he kept grinning at her, were things she could get used to. She liked this side of Craig Masters.

Suddenly, her marshmallow caught fire. Craig grabbed the stick and blew a strong breath against the flame. She could have done that herself, but she let him be chivalrous. Why not?

He dropped the burned marshmallow into the sand, then slid a fresh marshmallow onto her stick. She didn't need another one. But slow-roasting the sugary treat was fun. Holding the stick higher above the fire, she turned it slowly.

She met Craig's gaze again. He gave her a soft smile and settled back into his chair, watching her. Butterflies took flight in her stomach. Where was this going between them? Where did she want it to go?

"So, tell us, Alison," Paisley said, "what projects are you working on?"

Something tightened in Ali's chest. She didn't want to discuss work-related topics tonight.

"Al's work is hush, hush," Craig said before she had a chance to form a polite response.

"I told you not to call me that."

Paisley laughed. "Al, huh?"

"He called me that back in fifth grade the year my family stayed with Uncle Milton." She shrugged. "I hated it then. Still do."

"Even when I say it nicely?"

Craig's flirty tone buzzed through her sensors, sending out romantic alerts to every nerve ending. She needed to tone things down between them.

"Even then," she said with pseudo sternness.

A round of chuckles followed and a few more childhood tales were told.

Her marshmallow got droopy and fell off her stick, sizzling into the fire. She set the stick down. Then snuggled her coat tighter around her neck, blocking out the chilly night air. Above them, the stars were out in all their glory. "Wow," she said softly.

Craig leaned closer to her, gazing up also. "The sky above the ocean is something, isn't it?"

"I forgot how brilliant it is."

"Merry Christmas, Al."

His warm breath on her cheek, she turned to tell him one more time not to call her the silly nickname. But finding his eyes so near hers, his mouth close, the words died. When he tugged her toward him, his body blocking her from seeing Paisley and Judah, and kissed her cheek, she felt breathless.

"Thanks for coming out here with me tonight," he said quietly. "For having breakfast with me this morning. That was great too."

"Sure," she whispered. "I've enjoyed myself."

His gaze pinged between her lips and her eyes. Was he picturing kissing her on the mouth like she was doing? He wouldn't dare kiss her like that with Paisley and Judah looking on! If he did, what would she do? Kick him? Or melt into his arms?

The moment passed. Grinning, Craig sat back and drank from his tea bottle.

Ali's heart rate returned to normal. Or close to normal.

Paisley sang a Christmas song quietly, and Judah joined her. They sounded lovely singing together, hands clasped. How happy they must be knowing Paisley was pregnant. Especially after the ordeal she'd gone through with Edward kidnapping her.

Ali still wanted the chance to interview her, hearing the first-person story of her kidnapping and rescue. But she'd come to accept the woman wouldn't talk to her until after the trial, if then. Still, a humanitarian piece about how Paisley and Judah managed to cope in the aftermath of such a trauma at the hands of his father might be inspirational to her readers. Would Paisley allow an interview with a less threatening agenda?

Ali wouldn't bring up the story tonight. Even though her nature was to be pushy, the song Paisley and Judah were singing reached her heart with something undefinable. Peace, perhaps.

Craig's hand loosely clasped hers, and she didn't withdraw from his touch. Pulling away from holding a man's hand while a married couple, who'd gone through the worst of storms and survived, sang with their gazes lifted toward the sky felt irreverent.

The sound of "Oh, Holy Night" mixing with the sounds of the wind and the waves sent chills skidding over her. The air felt charged with holiness or majesty. Or pure perfection.

Tears filled her eyes, and she didn't fight them like she usually did. A few lyrics came out of her mouth, words she recalled from Sunday school or Christmas parties when she was a kid. Beneath the multitude of stars, with people who'd offered her friendship and acceptance, and yes, even holding Craig's hand, the words about a savior and faith and this special day made more sense.

Sixty-one

The day after Christmas Forest awoke to his phone buzzing. "Brian" displayed on the screen. He groaned. What did the deputy want this early in the morning?

He rolled over and sat up. Paige was already gone from their bed, probably painting.

"Hey," he answered the phone in a groggy voice. "What's going on?"

"Can you come into the office ASAP?" Deputy Brian asked in a demanding tone.

"Okay. What's going on?"

"I'll explain when you get here."

"Thirty minutes?" Forest would have preferred an hour.

"That works."

This wasn't how he imagined his morning after Christmas starting. He'd planned to meet up with his parents before they headed back to Portland. Teal and her boys would be sticking around for a few more days, which was good since he and his sister hadn't gotten a chance to chat by themselves.

He found Paige painting in the kitchen. "Morning, baby." He kissed her cheek.

"Hey, you." She set her paintbrush on the lip of the easel. "Was I too noisy?"

"Nah. My phone woke me." He tugged her into his arms, enjoying being close to his wife.

"Who was it?"

"Deputy Brian." Saying the man's name put his brain in work mode. What might the department want? Was Sheriff Morris upset about the newspaper article? Forest wouldn't mention that to Paige.

"Anything you can share?" She smoothed her palms over his T-shirt.

He wished he could stay home with her today. Relaxing with his wife, without any worries about work, would be his idea of a perfect day. But a job was a job. He should follow through with Deputy Brian's request.

"He didn't say what it's about, but he wants to talk with me about something." He kissed the side of her head, smelled the herbal scent of her hair. "Enjoy your painting time."

"Okay. Thanks."

He fixed a cup of coffee then made a beeline for the shower.

"Deputy," Forest said as he entered the small jail office, feeling more alert than when he took the call a half hour ago. "You wanted to see me?"

"Yep." Brian appeared to be working on an email or something requiring his full attention to the computer screen. He shoved away from the desk and stood. "Mia Till is missing."

"Missing? When did this happen?"

"She hasn't shown up for work in a week."

"A week?" Forest thought over his phone call to C-MER a few days ago. "Why didn't her employer report her missing before now?"

"It was the Christmas holidays." Brian strode to the coffee station, partially filled his cup, then dumped about a half-cup of creamer into it. "C.L. called this morning. His texts and calls to her have gone unanswered. Not like Mia to skip work." Brian's eyebrows shot up. "Or to ignore a single guy's attempts to contact her."

"You haven't seen her, either?"

Brian's cup stopped an inch from his lips. "Why would I have seen her?"

"I heard what she said to you. What she implied."

"I told you to forget that."

"Yeah, but you know things about her routine." Forest took a deep breath, calming his tone. "You told me she frequented Bert's for lunch. You nominated her for mayor."

"Let's not go down that rabbit trail again." Brian slurped his coffee, then wiped the back of his hand over his mouth. "I haven't talked to her since I questioned her about the books over a week ago." He took another swallow. "This is a high-priority assignment straight from Sheriff Morris."

"Okay, fine. What do you need me to do?" Forest's brain buzzed through a checklist. Access Mia's phone records. Follow her credit card details. Talk with C.L. and some of the guys at C-MER. Ask around town if anyone had seen her recently.

"I've put out an all-points statewide missing person bulletin." Brian shuffled his black shoe against the floor. "We need your detective skills out there immediately."

"I'll do my best."

"One other thing. The sheriff wants any data concerning Mia's correspondence with Edward and Evie."

"Oh?"

"Now that she's missing, he's suspicious of her previous activity with Edward." The deputy shrugged. "Do you think someone might be trying to silence her before the trial?"

"Why would they?"

"Who knows?"

Here Forest thought Mia might be complicit with Edward. Not a victim. "I'll get right on it. Maybe you should question Evie."

"I already plan to do that."

Forest left the deputy's office, his thoughts churning. Mia was missing? Seriously? What if this was all a ruse? What if she drove somewhere for the holidays and got detained? This concern for her might be all in vain. Then again, what if she had a car accident or met with foul play? What if the deputy was right and someone was trying to silence her before the trial?

Just as he reached his car, his phone rang. The contact display showed "Unknown." Tempted to let the call go unanswered, he tapped the screen. "Forest Harper."

"This is Alison Riley."

"Alison?" She was the last person on the planet he expected to call him.

"Sorry to call so early." She took a ragged breath. "I've written some unkind things about you. Things I was assured were correct. But if I discover I was wrong, I will write an honest retraction."

"Okay. Thanks." He hardly knew what to make of her impassioned speech. "What's this about?"

"I need your help ... as a detective, that is. My uncle is—" She huffed. "Look, I'm willing to pay you whatever it costs to get the information I need."

Forest frowned. He woke up jobless. Within one hour, two parties were interested in his investigative services? One of them being the same person who wrote negative things about him in the paper?

"What's going on?"

"Can you come by the newspaper office?"

He should go by Mia's apartment and have a look around first.

"Are you there now?" He could swing by on his way to Mia's and talk to Alison.

"I am."

"Be there in five."

Mia was missing *and* Alison Riley needed his help? What a strange start to his day.

Forest strode into the *Gazette* office and peered around the room filled with waist-high stacks of newspapers. How long had these been gathering here? The well-groomed journalist who ate dinner with the family on Christmas Eve, the one who wrote eloquently, albeit sometimes harshly, seemed a contradiction to this cluttered, unkempt room.

"Thank you for coming over so quickly." Alison wrung her hands, standing behind a counter piled with more papers.

"Of course. What did you want to see me about?"

"My uncle left town quickly and asked me to fill in for

him. He's a good man. An honest professional." Alison pressed her lips together, shaking her head. "Or so I thought."

"You think differently about him now?"

"I don't know what to think. Other than he's in trouble." Alison paced in the small space between the counter and an equally messy desk. "Maybe he did something wrong. Or pulled strings for someone he shouldn't have. But I'm worried sick about him."

Mentally, Forest categorized Alison's actions. Hands twisting together. Shifty glances around the room. Agitated pacing. Thrusting her hands through her hair. Seemed about to break emotionally.

"He's not missing, exactly," she said in a quieter tone.

"Not exactly?"

Either he was or he wasn't.

"He called me yesterday."

So, not missing.

"But he sounded under duress. He's hiding. Says he's being threatened."

"Threatened about what?" Forest pulled his pen and notepad out of his coat pocket. "What's his name?"

"Milton Hedge." Alison took a breath. "He was the one who gave me the data about you and told me to write the article. Now he says to close shop and leave town. I refused." Her words ran over each other revealing her stress level even more. "He's being framed, or something. He barely sounds like himself."

"What do you think it's all about?"

"The trial, what else?"

Forest stared hard at Alison. "Is he involved in Edward's trial?"

"Apparently. He says something bad may happen to him, or me, if he testifies."

"Someone's coercing him, then?" Forest jotted that down.

"It sounds like it." She thrust both hands over her hair, making it appear messier. "I'm scared too."

"What would you like me to do?"

"Find him. Look into why he fears for his life. For my life, too."

"Do you need a safe place to stay?" Maybe she could temporarily board with the ladies at the project house.

"Hard to say. I work here alone. Live in Uncle Milton's house. But he thinks they may come after me as leverage. Although, I don't know if he's thinking rationally." Her voice took on a desperate tone. "That's why I need you to find him."

"Any idea who 'they' are?"

"No. He suggested I look into why Mike Linfield left suddenly."

Forest wrote down the man's name, then pocketed the notepad and pen. "It's public knowledge, so I can tell you, someone else is missing."

"Who's that?"

"Mia Till."

"But she's—" Alison clenched her lips together. "Please find my uncle. I must see him."

"You should have someone else here with you. Don't be alone, okay?" Forest strode toward the door. "If anything comes to mind that you can tell me, you have my number. Lock this door after I leave."

"I won't sit still and do nothing," Ali called after him. "I'm going to pursue the truth."

"As will I."

He returned to his car with questions strumming through his brain. Did Milton's and Mike's departures have anything to do with Mia's disappearance? Anything to do with Edward's trial? Was Alison in any real danger?

Sixty-two

Craig left Bert's diner where the place was abuzz with news of Mia's disappearance. The way he heard it, Lucy took a breakfast plate to Evie at the jail like she usually did, and Deputy Brian asked if she'd seen Mia lately. According to Lucy's fast-spreading tale, no one had heard from Mia in days.

Was that why Craig hadn't gotten a response from her? Had something bad happened? Here Mia might be in danger, and he'd been thinking of her as a flake. That made him feel like a louse.

He shot her a text. *Where are you? Are you okay?*

A text from Forest flashed across his screen. *Can you hang out with Alison today? She may need some security.*

Security? She'd mentioned receiving a threat. Did Forest think it was viable? Enough for her to need someone watching out for her?

Sure, I can do that.

He'd rather be with Al than doing community service any day!

A short walk later, he rapped on the front door of the *Gazette* office. Al opened the door looking frazzled. Her hair poked up like she'd been raking her fingers through it.

He strode into the cluttered room. "How's it going?"

She shut the door and the lock clicked into place. "Not great." She sounded near tears.

Hearing her even slightly close to crying, he held out his arms to her. She lunged toward him, wrapping her arms around him tightly.

"Thanks for coming by. I needed a friendly face." Clearing her throat, she stepped back, her cheeks turning deep pink. Was she embarrassed by them hugging?

"You think my face is friendly, huh?"

"Don't push it. I see you're ready for work detail." She touched the word "jail" on his vest. "Even the day after Christmas, huh?" Her words lacked their usual barb.

"I just heard about Mia."

"I heard about her too." Stepping around a few paper stacks, she walked over to her desk. "What do you make of it?" She sat down.

"It's troubling." He followed her and dropped into the chair by her desk.

"I swallowed my pride and asked Forest to help me find my uncle. Now someone else is missing?"

"Everyone's talking about it at Bert's."

"Hopefully, Forest can find her. Uncle Milton, too." She drew in a shaky-sounding breath. "Maybe even Mike Linfield."

"What's this about Mike?" Craig scooted forward in his chair. "He was my boss at C-MER."

"Three people have left Basalt Bay suddenly and suspiciously. We have to find out why."

"Do they have anything in common?" Craig unzipped his vest. "Mike had a flaming temper primed to explode. It's no surprise he got the ax."

"Maybe. But what if we don't find out what's forcing these people out before it's too late?"

"Too late for what?"

"Before Edward's trial. Before someone coerces my uncle, Mike, or Mia to lie under oath." Al dropped her hands into her lap. "Or before whatever the dirty scoundrels have planned for the town happens."

Now she sounded paranoid. But Craig would do anything for her, stay with her, protect her, whatever. "You said your uncle keeps everything he's written, correct?" He waved his right hand toward a stack of musty newspapers.

"Everything. His house looks just like this. Papers everywhere."

"I have an idea." He stood and slipped out of his vest and raincoat. He pushed up the sleeves of his navy button-up shirt, ready to get down to business. "If Milton kept every newspaper, let's read everything he published over the last year or two and see where the paper trail leads."

"You're serious?" She stood quickly and strode around the desk. "You'd do that with me?"

"However long it takes, I'm here for you." He clasped both of her hands and gave a slight squeeze. "Forest thinks you might need security."

She jerked her hands away from his. "I don't need any man watching over me."

"No? How about someone who cares about you and wants you to stay safe?"

"You mean like a friend?"

"Sure. Like that."

However, gazing deeply into her eyes, he felt more than a casual interest in protecting her or in being just her friend. Like a magnet to steel, his gaze zeroed in on her shiny red lips. She moistened the edge of her mouth with her tongue, then gnawed on her lower lip, and he was a goner. He leaned slightly toward her.

Wait. Al didn't need him pushing for a relationship right now. He stepped back, controlling his desire to forget searching for her uncle and kiss her into the next year.

"Let's, uh"—he cleared his throat—"try to figure out what those scums you mentioned have been planning to do. Maybe your uncle wrote something about them. I have a hunch there's a connection tying Edward, Mia, Evie, and whoever is threatening Milton, together. I'd ask my mom, but she's lied to me for years. I doubt she'd tell me the truth now." He nodded toward a pile of papers. "I'll start over here."

Al stepped between two stacks, blocking his attempt to get through the maze. "Thank you, Craig." She kissed his cheek lightly. "You are my one true friend in Basalt Bay."

Too bad she didn't think of him as more than that. Yet, friends was a good starting place.

Since she was blocking his way, he still couldn't move forward. In fact, her glistening gaze aimed at him seemed to be sending him romantic signals, not friendship vibes. His heart pounded like a runner guzzling an energy drink.

Al's red lips spread in a flirty smile, and he did what he'd been thinking about doing a lot lately. He leaned toward her, gauging her reaction, even pausing to see if she'd pull away. When she didn't, he let his lips skim hers briefly. Just a taste, a bare movement of his mouth against hers. A powerful jolt hit him.

He stumbled back, wouldn't take advantage of her vulnerability. He was here to help her. To be a friend, if that's what she needed him to be. "I'm here for you, Al."

"I told you not to—"

"Don't waste your breath. You'll always be Al to me."

Everything within him wanted to take her in his arms and kiss her like a man who was crazy in love. *Love?* Did he love Al? Was it possible he cared for her that much?

"Always?" she asked uncertainly.

"Yeah. Always."

She chuckled. "We'll see about that."

"Oh, yes, we will."

For now, they had papers to search through, a possible trail of information to scour, and Al's uncle to find. Craig didn't know what they were looking for, but he wanted to do something helpful for Al, Mia, Paisley, even for Forest. Maybe in the process, he'd help bring the unrest in Basalt Bay to an end. Would that make up for his own wrongdoings of the past?

Sixty-three

With a streak of early morning light coming through the attic window, Ruby sat on the edge of the bed, putting on her shoes. She tried not to make any noise that might wake up Peter. They'd been back together for a week, sleeping as husband and wife, sharing in deep conversations and laughter. In some ways, it felt like they were getting to know each other all over again.

"Hey, Rube." His deep throaty voice brushed across her senses, making her want to curl back up in his arms.

"Morning. Sorry if I awakened you."

"Why are you leaving me so early?"

She chuckled. "I'm ready for coffee. Want some?"

"You know I do."

He clasped her hand and tugged her to him. Laughing, she fell against his chest, but only for one sweet kiss.

"Be right back," she whispered.

"I'm holding you to that." He closed his eyes as if he were going to doze back to sleep.

She slipped away and went down the ladder.

In the darkened kitchen, she saw a figure huddled at the center island. She froze, her heart hammering. Hadn't Forest warned them to be on the lookout for anything suspicious? Then, detecting sniffles, not anything dangerous, she flicked on the light.

Sarah sat on a stool, her face wet and red, and in her hands, she clutched an empty mug so tightly her knuckles had turned white. How long was she sitting here like this?

"Sarah, are you okay?" Ruby dropped onto a stool beside her. "Did you have a bad dream again?"

"Yes." She wiped her sweatshirt sleeve over her face.

A couple of nights ago, Ruby used the bathroom and heard crying coming from Sarah's bedroom. She tapped on the door and asked if she was all right. That was when Sarah told her she was suffering from nightmares.

"Anything you want to talk about?"

"Not really. I want to forget the image of my husband's car wreck. But I can't—" She cried into her hands.

"Oh, Sarah." Ruby smoothed her palm over her shoulder. "Can I get you anything? Tea or more coffee? I was about to fix some for Peter and me."

"No thanks." Sarah lowered her hands and sniffed. "Today would have been our ... tenth anniversary. That's why I'm such a mess."

Ruby wrapped her arms around her. "I'm so sorry. This must be a terribly hard day for you."

"It is." She sniffled. "You've been a good friend. What will I do when you leave?"

"Are you worried about that?" Ruby settled back on the stool.

"Uh-huh."

"You'll be okay. You and Kathleen get along well, don't you?"

"We do."

Ruby sat with Sarah for a few minutes, silently asking God to heal her broken heart.

Hearing a noise behind her, she turned. Peter leaned against the doorframe, his arms crossed in a relaxed pose, his hair sticking up in tufts. His gaze traveled from Ruby to Sarah, then back again, as if taking in the situation.

"I was worried when you didn't come back with my coffee."

"Sorry. We got to talking—"

"And you forgot about your husband?" he asked teasingly.

"Not quite." She grinned at him. "Do you still want me to fix your coffee?"

She glanced at Sarah. How was she handling Peter and Ruby's interactions? Was watching them being even mildly flirtatious difficult for her, considering today's anniversary date?

"I'll grab a mug myself. Morning, Sarah." Peter shuffled past them toward the coffeemaker.

"Good morning." Sarah lifted her cup. "Coffee was good."

"Can't wait for my first three cups."

"First three?" Sarah's eyes widened.

Ruby grinned. "He won't be finished until he's consumed five or six cups."

"You know me well." Peter winked at her.

The warm way he gazed at her heated up Ruby's cheeks. Yes, she knew him well. And loved him completely.

Sarah chuckled, which seemed like a good sign that she was feeling a bit better.

"What are your plans for the day?" Ruby asked. "Keeping yourself busy might be a way to get through the tough parts."

"Kathleen offered to show me how to do mosaics."

"That sounds great. If I weren't heading back to Alaska, I'd want to learn too."

"I, for one, am glad you're coming home with me," Peter said in a husky tone. He brushed a kiss across Ruby's cheek. "Are you coming back upstairs?"

"I am. See you in a few minutes."

Their gazes met again.

He sipped his steaming black coffee and sauntered toward the doorway. Glancing back over his shoulder, he smiled at her.

Ah, Peter.

Having him back in her life, having him living here in the project house with her, were answers to her prayers. Soon they'd be heading north to begin the next chapter of their lives together. While it was too soon to know, she was already hoping for the chance to tell him about a new addition to their family.

She was so thankful she came to Basalt Bay in search of answers. And that Peter followed her here. What would have happened if he hadn't come after her? Would they even be together now?

"Ruby? Go with him." Sarah nodded toward the doorway. "I'm sad, but I'll be fine. Take every opportunity to be together. Enjoy being in love with your husband."

"I will." Ruby nodded. "Thank you for reminding me."

"Of course. Someday I hope to find what you've found, again, too."

"I'll be praying with you for that." Ruby squeezed her hand.

"Thank you. Now, go."

Laughing, Ruby stood and fixed a tray with two mugs of coffee—one for her, and another one for Peter—and two pastries. Then she headed up to the attic. For today, for right now, nothing else in the world mattered as much as being with her sweet husband.

Thank you for reading *Sound of Rejoicing*, Part 7 in the Restored series!

Look for *Shores of Resilience*, the 8th and final Part in the Restored series, in June 2022.

Books by Mary Hanks

Restored Series

Ocean of Regret
Sea of Rescue
Bay of Refuge
Tide of Resolve
Waves of Reason
Port of Return
Sound of Rejoicing
Shores of Resilience (June '22)

Second Chance Series

Winter's Past
April's Storm
Summer's Dream
Autumn's Break
Season's Flame

Thank you *to everyone who helped make this book possible!*

Paula McGrew—You've been such a blessing to my writer's journey. Thank you for guiding my words and storyline. And for your positivity and encouragement throughout the whole process! I'm so thankful for you!

Suzanne Williams—I appreciate your artistry and help with this cover design and all the others. Thank you for helping me see my dreams come true.

Kellie Griffin, Mary Acuff, Beth McDonald, Joanna Brown, and Jason Hanks—Thank you for continuing with this series and reading Book 7! Your encouragement and guidance in my writer's journey means so much to me. Thank you for commenting on what you like and what you hope to see in future stories. God bless you!

My family—Jason, Daniel & Traci, Philip, Deborah, Shem, & Lala-girl—I love you forever!

The Lord—who blesses me with fun ideas for stories!

(This is a work of fiction. Any mistakes are my own. ~meh)

About Mary Hanks

Mary loves stories about marriage reconciliation. She believes there's something inspiring about couples clinging to each other, working through their problems, and depending on God for a beautiful rest of their lives together. Those are the types of stories she likes to write.

Besides writing and reading, Mary enjoys gardening, doing mosaics, going on adventures with Jason, and meeting up for coffee with her four adult kids.

Connect with Mary by signing up for her newsletter at

www.maryehanks.com

"Like her Facebook Author page:

www.facebook.com/MaryEHanksAuthor

Thank you for reading the Restored series!

www.maryehanks.com